Goodbye, Wisconsin

Works by Glenway Wescott

Novels
The Apple of the Eye, 1924
The Grandmothers, 1927
The Pilgrim Hawk, 1940
Apartment in Athens, 1945

Short Stories
Goodbye, Wisconsin, 1928

Single Stories Published in Book Form
Like a Lover, 1926
The Babe's Bed, 1930
A Visit to Priapus, 1995

Poetry
The Bitterns, 1920
Natives of Rock, 1925

Essays
Fear and Trembling, 1932
Images of Truth, 1962

Journals
Continual Lessons: The Journals of Glenway
    Wescott 1937–55, 1990

Miscellaneous
A Calendar of Saints for Unbelievers, 1932
Twelve Fables of Aesop: Newly Narrated by
    Glenway Wescott, 1954

Goodbye, Wisconsin

Glenway Wescott

With an Introduction by Jerry Rosco

Illustrated by Steve Chappell

> "Beside this temple dedicated to Fear, the
> Lacedaemonians have others consecrated
> to Death, Laughter, and similar powers.
> They honor Fear, not as a baleful spirit to
> be propitiated, but because they regard it
> as the chief support of their body politic."
> –Plutarch, *Agis and Cleomenes*

Borderland Books

Borderland Books Edition 2008

Copyright ©1928 by Harper & Brothers
Copyright © renewed 1955 by Glenway Wescott

Introduction copyright ©2008 by Borderland Books

Woodblock prints copyright ©2008 by Steve Chappell

Published by Borderland Books, Madison, Wisconsin
www.borderlandbooks.net

Published by arrangement with the Estate of Glenway Wescott, Anatole Pohorilenko, literary executor, c/o Harold Ober Associates, Inc., New York, New York.

Publisher's Cataloging-in-Publication Data

Wescott, Glenway, 1901–1987.

Goodbye, Wisconsin / Glenway Wescott; with an introduction by Jerry Rosco; illustrated by Steve Chappell.

p. : ill. ; cm.

ISBN: 978-0-9768781-7-9

1. United States—Social life and customs—20th century—Fiction. 2. Short stories. I. Rosco, Jerry. II. Chappell, Steve, 1963– . III. Title.

PS3545.E827 G66 2008

813/.54   2008922545

Printed in the United States of America

Contents

Introduction
by Jerry Rosco

These stories and the introductory essay were written in the 1920s, the most exciting time of Glenway Wescott's life. When *Goodbye, Wisconsin* first appeared in 1928, he was at the high point of his early fame, right alongside fellow midwesterners and expatriates Ernest Hemingway and F. Scott Fitzgerald. A year earlier his second novel, *The Grandmothers,* was a huge success, a classic great American novel, gilded by Wescott's jewel-like prose and exquisite sensitivity. It was also a model of the family chronicle in fiction, and has been reprinted many times.

While there are similarities with the individual tales that largely make up *The Grandmothers,* the stories in *Goodbye, Wisconsin* are different. They draw from the same rich vein of midwestern material, but half of them were written in the mid-twenties and with a few exceptions are not autobiographical. The characters in this book range from tragic to heroic, comic to sinister, sympathetic to strange. At times it reminds one of Sherwood Anderson's *Winesburg, Ohio,* but there is the great contrast of Wescott's poetic style, swift intellect, and aphoristic commentary. These stories are the fiction writer's rendering of real stories, rumors, gossip, and local legend. But there is also the perspective that the individual writer brings to his work. In Wescott that includes respect for Midwest courtesy and decency, but also animosity toward the old-fashioned puritanism that stifles creativity and humanity. It includes a love of the landscape even when it is impoverished, and of nature even when it is cruel. After all, Wescott came from real poverty, from a small farm in Kewaskum, Wisconsin, and made his way to the University of Chicago on a scholarship at sixteen. After three semesters, his college days ended when the Spanish flu of 1919 devastated the Chicago area and nearly killed him. He survived, met his great lifelong friend Monroe Wheeler, and made his way to New York and Europe. Eventually, his close friendships would include many of the great names in the arts. In society, he'd be a welcome guest of the Rockefellers, Astors, and Rothschilds. But he never forgot where he came from, or stopped loving it. That he had a home on his brother's farm in western New Jersey was very important to him. The novelist and *New Yorker* editor William Maxwell said of Wescott, "When he reached for a metaphor, it came, like him, out of rural Wisconsin."

The title essay that introduces the stories is very interesting to anyone curious about Wescott in that moment of time, the late 1920s, when he'd had all that success in Europe and returned to America to visit his family for the winter holidays. It's also interesting as a clear, candid look at a small midwestern town then. The exact timing would be December 1927, the Christmas before this book's first publication. That month, a *New York Herald Tribune* review of his prize novel was entitled "A Celebrity at Twenty-Seven" (four months early with his age). But as you'll see in his essay here, on a train heading north from Milwaukee he finds it awkward explaining to curious workmen that he's coming from Chicago, and before that was visiting New York — and doesn't bother adding that he's really visiting from Paris. "If this were Europe, I would have told them I was a writer, which would have been the end of it."

His father had given up the farm in Kewaskum for a home in Ripon — called Claron in the essay — in hope of finding work. When Wescott arrives he finds their house has a few improvements over the farmhouse of his youth but is still brutally cold at night. As for the town, Wescott's observations are like those of his autobiographical character, Alwyn Tower, in parts of *The Grandmothers*. The small town movie theater serves as "the imagination's chapel." He notes the uneasy politics of the town church, whose pastor has to balance his role with his finances. While he's met midwesterners all around the world, he wonders about those determined to stay at home: "They ask question after question and prefer not to take advice." Transportation and population had changed Wisconsin from the wilderness he knew as a boy—now even farmhands were influenced by popular culture as observed in the nearest town. As his visit ends and he leaves for the world that awaits him in New York and Europe, he reflects on the mystery of the Midwest: "It is a certain climate, a certain landscape, and beyond that it is a state of mind."

Like the essay "Goodbye, Wisconsin," which first appeared in *The New York Herald Tribune Books*, most of the stories here were also published in periodicals and anthologies. The earlier ones weren't written by a successful celebrity author, but by a small journal poet and reviewer in his early twenties who was attempting more ambitious fiction writing. Thanks to the influence of Yvor Winters, Janet Lewis, and others from the Poetry Club of the University of Chicago, Wescott did show talent as an Imagist poet. His early reviews showed great depth and intelligence—no surprise to those who knew of the tremendous amount of reading he'd already done in his teens. By the time his long story "Bad Han" appeared in *The Dial*, he'd already expanded the manuscript into his first novel, *The Apple of the Eye*. But he was also writing some of the short fiction you find here.

"In a Thicket" appeared in *The Dial* that same year, 1924, and would be selected for *The Best Short Stories of* 1924. The story of a young girl who lives with her deeply religious grandfather has a mysterious edge to it. Perhaps feeling isolated by his excessive Christian fervor, she keeps secret a chilling, nighttime danger to herself and him, and somehow survives it, by a protective force that can't be explained. It would later appear in two French publications and a British anthology.

"The Runaways" was originally published as "This Way Out." Wescott had actually made a draft of it during his first trip to Europe in 1922, and put it aside. After *The Apple of the Eye* received nothing but rave reviews, he was given a small advance on a second novel, plus a patron's gift, and left with Monroe Wheeler for France in early 1925. This time it wasn't to visit or tour Europe on a slim budget, but to actually live among the expatriates while he worked on his next book. Any money he could add to their funds was very important. A few months after he arrived in France, he wrote a friend to say he'd sold a story for "an enormous sum" to *Collier's National Weekly*. It would also appear in *The Best Short Stories of 1925* as "Fire and Ice," and later in a modern literature anthology. No doubt, the appeal of the story is that it is so strange that it feels all too true. A shiftless young couple can't make a living off their poor farm and have a hare-brained scheme to get insurance money. When that fails they run away and literally join a circus, and in a bizarre way their world suddenly makes sense.

In Wescott's journals, *Continual Lessons*, he remembers when he and Wheeler escorted novelist Katherine Anne Porter and other friends to Coney Island in 1937. For Wescott, the 1930s were tough years of writing block and aborted novels. But as he and Wheeler walked Porter through Coney Island amusement park, with its rides, games, and shooting gallery, Wheeler made Wescott smile by recalling their youthful triumph, the *Collier's* story: "It reminds me of 'The Runaways,'" he said.

"Adolescence" stands out as the most autobiographical story in the collection, and therefore the one Wescott liked to talk about. The main characters are a thirteen-year-old poor farmboy and his friend from school, a fifteen-year-old from a well-to-do family in town. Carl, the older boy, was Philip's protector and hero. When they are invited to a masquerade party, it is Carl who suggests that his sisters dress Philip as a girl, with a mask to complete the disguise. There's lots of room for rich ambiguity in this story told from the perspective of Wescott's autobiographical character, Philip. The social contrast of a poor rural youth at a party of his comfortably middle-class schoolmates is interesting enough. So is the unsettled sexuality of all youngsters in their mid-teens. And the story lightly touches on the deeper level of Wescott's real-life experience. The older friend in real life was named Earl, and his sexual relationship with Glenway lasted more than a year, until he discovered girls. In the copy of *Goodbye, Wisconsin* that Glenway gave me, he wrote on the blank page before the story: "The earliest communication at my big wild archive—at Haymeadows, not in the Berg [his Rosemont, New Jersey, farmhouse, not the New York Public Library's Berg Collection]—is a postcard dated September 1914, addressed to my mother, telling her that I wanted to stay in West Bend that weekend in order to go to this party disguised as a girl. I was thirteen; 'Carl,' whom I had indefatigably induced to take my virginity, was fifteen."

In the story, Philip does not like wearing women's clothes, but it is in disguise from his world that he finds himself. Abandoned by his friend, seemingly invisible to the others, he becomes thoughtful about his life, no longer willing to be a child, determined to become independent. Like James Joyce's "Araby," this is an enduring story of adolescence.

"A Guilty Woman" takes an odd twist. A schoolteacher who murdered an abusive lover comes out of prison with one friend in the world, a widower who offers her a temporary home. And by chance or fate she hurts that friend and is left feeling guilty in a different way. The story was printed numerous times, including in *The Best Short Stories of 1928.* It's not important to the story but it is interesting that the teacher recalls one of her former students sending her letters and magazines while she was in prison—Philip, Wescott's fictional self in the previous story. Also, decades later it must have seemed ironic to Wescott that his brother Lloyd's notable public work and titles included board member of a local women's prison. And at their farm they employed two former prisoners, murderers, who became cherished longtime members of the household.

In all Wescott's fiction of the Midwest, there is the underlying tension of his humanitarianism and agnostic instincts versus an often harsh brand of Christianity. He makes it the central issue in "The Dove Came Down," where a man and his fiancée attend church services, partly to escape their relatives. With no action but the church routine and the walk afterward, this is a fine example of the sort of interior writing at which Wescott excels. All the movement of the story is in their conversation and his thoughts. For her, religion is something emotional and mysterious. He simply believes that life is difficult and the best virtue is in personal strength and stoicism. So, even before marriage, this great divide had to be accepted and left unresolved. Each person must be true to his or her ultimate belief.

Another of the earlier-written stories is "Like a Lover." Monroe Wheeler published it as a deluxe chapbook in France in 1926, and it later appeared in a French journal. Like the chilling mystery of "In a Thicket," there is a dark undercurrent here. Despite warnings, two women, years apart, can't help being drawn to a man who has a violent, even homicidal nature.

The remaining stories, written when *The Grandmothers* was fully drafted, continue the strong storytelling but perhaps with a sharper edge. "Prohibition" is set in the atmosphere of the Protestant temperance movement, just before the 1920–1933 law banning alcohol. Local drunks like Old Riley caused constant problems in farming communities and small towns, and for their wives and families. In this case, Old Riley becomes a "moral lesson of the ridiculous," his misfortune a tragedy with a happy ending. Linking two stories in a direct way, Wescott tells the story of Old Riley's younger son, Terrie, in "The Sailor." Before moving to Paris in late 1928, Wescott spent his first three expatriate years in Villefranche, near Nice, completing *The Grandmothers* and these stories. Dedicated to expatriate Mary Reynolds, "The Sailor" evokes the colorful port town where he knew Jean Cocteau and dozens of other writers and artists. In fact, years later F. Scott Fitzgerald wrote Wescott to say that Hemingway told him that Wescott's description of the Villefranche harbor in "The Sailor" sounded similar to Fitzgerald's description in his forthcoming novel, *Tender Is the Night*. Fitzgerald decided that the similarities couldn't be avoided. In the story, Terrie returns to the farm from the Navy, but only to visit. His older brother understands that much, as he performs farm work while listening to Terrie's wild stories, and notices his appearance. Terrie has gotten tattoos, and he wears his belt down on his hips rather than on his waist (eighty years before the popularity of low-cut jeans). The sailor tells his silent brother about his months stationed in Villefranche. After knowing many women, he settled for a steady girlfriend—but soon she had a girlfriend, and the two girls liked "snow," cocaine. This subject matter shows that Wescott in the late-1920s was no longer the same author who wrote the early stories in this volume. Between the two brothers there is a great unspoken unease. The older brother finally says that Terrie would only get in trouble if he tried to stay and live in Wisconsin. The truth is that Terrie isn't half as wild as the girl he left behind—but he can't imagine living among people who can't understand him.

While most of the stories here appeared in periodicals in the same time period, "The Sailor" reappeared much later, in *American Harvest* in 1941, and in a sensational 1955 pulp paperback, *Crazy Mixed-up Kids,* alongside stories by Denton Welch, Shirley Jackson, William Faulkner, Jean-Paul Sartre, and others. One footnote would be the story's mention of a Villefranche bar with a framed poster of a woman "with blushing breasts and flowers in her hair, a sort of patron saint"—that would be Wescott's tragic friend from nearby Nice, the dancer Isadora Duncan.

Another very impressive late story, "The Wedding March" progresses on two levels, present and past: the church wedding of Hugo Randolph and his memory of a youthful relationship from fifteen years earlier that is troubling his heart. He'd had an affair with a married woman, which in his passionate youth meant everything. But ultimately she remained faithful to her husband, even in a marriage without passion. This double-story, describing the crossroads of a good man's life, is brilliantly executed.

This volume closes with "The Whistling Swan," which is fiction in its core but, I believe, draws from some very autobiographical moments and emotions. For a story of its kind at that time in mainstream American literature, it's daring and almost shocking. It is possible to read and appreciate this story without seeing the powerful undercurrent of homosexual theme—especially in the 1920s. One can see it simply as the battle between artistic freedom and middle-class compromise. But it's very easy to see much more. Hubert, a talented young composer and pianist, has been living and working in Paris, mostly through the patronage of a Chicago banker. When he is summoned home for a "visit," the banker's flamboyant male secretary prepares him for what's coming. Apparently, the patron has had less than an innocent relationship with Hubert and/or his other aspiring young artists. When the banker's wife visited Paris, she drew some conclusions after meeting Hubert and some of his friends. This added fuel to some conclusions about her husband. When confronted, her husband made Hubert the sacrificial lamb. The pompous hypocrite lectures Hubert about his questionable lifestyle in Paris and cuts off financial support. When Hubert then visits his parents in Wisconsin, he's faced with hard choices. He could try to get patronage from another source to return to Paris, but it would be difficult. Or he could accept a teaching position in Wisconsin, and perhaps marry the girl who loves him, though for him it is a platonic love. The white swan at the end symbolizes his creative and personal/sexual freedom.

Autobiographical links are clear. Like Wescott's parents, Hubert's parents had moved from a failed farm to a town, seeking better success. Like Hubert's long-distance girlfriend, Muriel, Kathleen Foster of the Chicago Poetry Club shared love letters and poems with Wescott, and they were engaged for a time. The story keenly reveals Wescott's own guilty feelings about the confused relationship of his early twenties with Kathleen. And while Wescott never had Hubert's awkward situation with a patron, he remembered being lectured about his lifestyle in 1928 by American music critic Katherine Lane. He told her, "I'm as shocked by your attitude as you are by me." And in 1922, he'd had to smooth over some gossip with an important Chicago supporter, Harriet Moody (widow of the poet

William Vaughn Moody). Unlike tragic Hubert, not to mention the poor swan, Wescott was lucky. At the time he wrote this story he was among the top five American writers, with no need for patrons or unhappy compromises.

Aside from the individual stories, the larger significance of *Goodbye, Wisconsin* is that it—along with the 1930 deluxe, encased long story *The Babe's Bed*—marked the end of Wescott's midwestern fiction. That early, prolific, unique work is enough to secure his place in our literature. Luckily, there is much more. After the unsuccessful 1930s, he wrote a 1940 short novel set in expatriate Paris, *The Pilgrim Hawk*, which is widely acknowledged as one of the great novellas in English. His 1945 bestseller, *Apartment in Athens*, is one of the best of the World War II novels. Aside from English editions, those two novels have been published in many foreign translations in recent years. He was a fine essayist, writing about literature (*Images of Truth*, 1962) and art, with a high place for his late, personal essays. Some readers enjoy his journals best (*Continual Lessons*, 1990), and I'm assembling his late journals now.

After the original edition by Harper & Brothers in 1928, *Goodbye, Wisconsin* was published in a British edition (Jonathan Cape, 1929), as a pulp paperback (Signet, 1964), and in a library edition (Books for Libraries Press, 1970). What every quality writer wants and deserves is simply that his books are available. As part of Glenway Wescott's remarkable life and work, *Goodbye, Wisconsin* is very important, and this handsome edition is cause for celebration.

Goodbye, Wisconsin

To Mrs. Walter Weil

Goodbye, Wisconsin

Homeward bound at last, north from Milwaukee on Christmas Eve. The red-towered station looks very German. But the stern, tattered, tall twilight is American; little by little it will change the German faces; and all that in the near future we can hope for, or fear, is resemblance. There used to be a saintly Scotchwoman in the waiting room to keep country girls from getting into trouble. In the train-shed the crowd surges against a high picket fence, sways in one piece like a boxcarful of cattle: a mixed population, returning to maternal arms, infant arms, arms in love. As the train moves north a blizzard comes south.

My life of the rest of the year being left behind, being buried beneath new impressions, trampled underfoot by resurrected ones, passing through and out of my head, bit by bit... The stiff carnations of the Mediterranean are in bloom. Never live in Paris: everyone there has done some harm to everyone else; the heart must be kept in fashion, there was the influence of Henry James, so it is no longer elegant to quarrel; they go on dining together, a malicious intimacy with a lump in its throat. In mid-Atlantic, a short rainbow alongside of the ship with both feet in the sea. Never live in New York either: a town in which "it is as essential to wear one's heart on one's sleeve as one's tongue in one's cheek." New York is halfway between the south of France and Wisconsin, always halfway between any two such places; that is its importance...

3

The train jerks, because the cars are of steel, I suppose. Oranges and green plush. The heat of a Turkish bath into which, through opening doors, through double windowpanes, the awful wind penetrates; nature and a comfort-loving race between them have made this the worst climate in the world. Somewhere up ahead everyone's Christmas tree, squat and dazzling.

A wild-looking youngster asks if anyone has seen his wife and baby. An old man watches over a girl as lovely as a film star. She wears in her hat a tied ostrich plume which looks as if long tresses of hair had grown on a stem; no other woman in the car is unfashionably dressed. She is a half-wit, and keeps eating sandwiches with the impressive ferocity of a monkey, clutching them with both hands. Here and there, students on their way home from college. Middle-class young men in France are less fine physically. Heads almost uniformly well-proportioned; the relaxed look that experts in dissimulation have when they are alone. Either they are blush-pink or they have that translucent dead-leaf skin, without yellowness, without whiteness, which seems peculiar to America and is said to be increasingly common, a result of American air, of the way of life and the climate. The mad girl has it, too.

Throbbing on the rails, the train begins running downhill, which means, I remember from childhood, that we have passed a town called Marblehead. That name and the mature schoolboys make me think of Greece—many-headed, marble-headed. France is its heir, eldest son in this generation of nations. I am jealous of every national glory. Not that I expect my country to become a poets' colony, a sculptors', architects', and moralists' colony. There were all sorts of Greeks… Heads of all complexions, even in the sculptured stone: ruddy and ivory and the very vivid brown—as if red rose-leaves had been tanned and made into a leather—which some of my friends, visiting the Mediterranean beaches, find objectionable and others do their best to acquire.

I have to change trains. The snowstorm is over, or we have passed through it. I share a corner of what is called a milk-train with a lot of baggage and two young workmen. One seems unhealthy: large hands bright with chemicals. The other has that look of sheepish melancholy which I frivolously associate with socialism. They engage in conversation about their jobs and each other's relatives which they know by name; their fathers are farmers; the yellow-handed one works in a tannery in Fond du Lac, the other is an ironworker in a Milwaukee foundry. They speak a mixture of several kinds of English — Swedish, German, Polish, Irish — immigrants' children of the second generation having inherited accents from all their parents at once, all the accents. They keep looking at my cigarette-lighter, my gloves, my tight black cap, a Basque beret.

The tanner: "Where d'ya work in Mulwauky?"

"I came up from Chicago."

"Yuh got some folks here?"

"My father and mother live in Claron. He was a farmer until he moved to town."

A pause, without embarrassment on their parts. The ironworker: "Wha' d'ya work at'n Chicago?"

"I don't work in Chicago. I've been in New York." I see myself retreating right round the world …

So I offer them cigarettes; they look at the mark; and out of timidity I open Thomas Mann's *Hochstapler Krull*. If this were Europe I could have told them that I was a writer, which would have been the end of it. One day years ago when I was wearing a rather pretentious black cape, I tipped a porter in a Munich railway station. "Thank you kindly, Herr poet," he said.

The train is making up for lost time. I know, I say to myself, what the country is like beyond the syncopated noise, the shaken light-bulbs, outside the sooty windows in the dark. The state with a beautiful name — glaciers once having made of it their pasture — is an anthology, a collection of all the kinds of landscape, perfect examples side by side. Ranges of hills strung from the great lake to the Mississippi River in long, lustrous necklaces, one above another from the northern throat of the state until well below

its waist. Peacock lakes of bronze weeds and vivid water, with
steep shores; four or five of them to be seen at a time from certain
hilltops. Fertility and wilderness in rapid succession along powdery
highways: classic meadows where the cattle seem to walk and eat
in their sleep, sandy slopes full of foxes, ledges where there are
still rattlesnakes. Sad forests full of springs; the springs have a
feverish breath. There are metallic plants which burn your hands
if you touch them. All summer the horizon trembles, hypnotically
flickering over the full grain, the taffeta corn, and the labor in them
of dark, over-clothed men, singing women, awe-stricken children.
These say nothing; their motionless jaws give an account of their
self-pity, dignity, and endurance. Sheet-lightning at night, and
they sleep in the grass, in hammocks, on folded blankets on the
floor—the beds are too hot. They get up and work with strange,
ardent motions and the obstinacies of ghosts in the heat; there is
wealth in it. In the sky mocking marble palaces, an Eldorado of
sterile cloud. Not sterile—for down fall large black-and-blue rains,
tied with electric ribbons; they never seem to be doing much good,
but the crops are saved...

Thus, neglecting the masterpiece which I keep in my hand to
prevent the workmen from asking questions but not uninfluenced
by its mood of shameless, summery confession—in which the true
nature of Herr Krull is almost obscured by the bright light shed
on every detail—I think of the land outside the train window as
one of perpetual summer. Then the door swings open; the blown
cold pounds on the nape of my neck; in spite of the coal-gas,
the tobacco, the oranges, the opium-sweetness of warm bodies, I
imagine that I can smell snow.

For in reality this is a sort of winter resort for storms from the
North Pole; now all the half tropic vegetation, the flesh and the
fruitfulness, stripped and lying quite still, are theirs. You seem
to be on a lofty plateau, and you can see with your own eyes
that the world is convex. The villages are almost as lonely as the
farms. It is like Russia with vodka prohibited and no stationary
peasantry—strictly speaking, with none at all. The soul hibernates

in the cold body; your feet ache for months at a time. I remember, at church, in my childhood, prayers that were visible, white and tenuous, and moustaches covered with frost through which the slow, discouraging hymn made its way. A good many men get drunk a great deal of the time in spite of everything. Once a month the new moon sets out like the crooked knife of a fairy story in search of a heart to bury itself in. This is the dying-season for old men and women. When the moon is full, over the crusted snow, men go rabbit-hunting...

The train stops at a junction and makes its presence known; with another lowing, female sound, another train replies. I have a vague remembrance of that junction, those two deep voices. I ask, and am told that we are coming into Claron.

Out of the dark run forward my young father, my small mother. Across the town in an automobile, no distance at all; home, the new house, a home in a town. On the small square of property close-pressed by other houses, collies with no more herds to tend; the color of pheasants with ruffled plumage, under the arc-light, against the snow-banks. Up the icy steps; a tumult in the doorway; energetic kisses which smell good, smell of health and warm wool; my brother, my sisters. Their courtesy a little affected but with burning eyes, breaking down repeatedly in the stress of the exuberance which they have in common, the stress of joy or disappointment, pride, contention, yearning. This is the wild fountain of friendliness. Sometimes it occurs to me that I ought to play the Ancient Mariner, but I am evidently always to be wedding guest.

There are chocolates and fruit; I remember the annual basket of grapes which my father used to bring from the state fair when we were children, a wooden basket with a wire handle and pale, elongated California grapes—each of us ate his share grape by grape, there were so few. The floors are waxed; carpets like everyone else's have taken the place of the rag rugs accumulated by my grandmothers. That fruitful, severe farmhouse of childhood, it seemed to have an immortal soul and now seems to have borne a physical resemblance to my mother—a house so cold at this time of the year that every vessel which held water had a lip of crystal. Here there is a bathroom. Progress, I think sleepily. The king is dead, long live the king; deprivation is dead ... I rejoice, but regret some of his poetry. Fortunately, progress has not gone far enough here to deprive me of a cold bed, of the drug of zero weather, the barbaric luxury of frost, in my nostrils all night long.

Early in the morning I go out to look at the town. It is like any other not too new or too large or too small in the state—or perhaps in any state not too far east or west. Main Street down the middle—beef-red brick and faded clapboards; it is lamentably impressive. The new banks, I must admit, are of lighter brick and adorned with brief, reasonably Roman pillars. The churches have an atheistic look and must have been very cheap to build. Dry-goods stores remarkably full of luxury; drug stores which sell everything (at a glance everything seems made of paper), the most expensive cameras and the cheapest books; a windowful of superb apples. Apples are wealth in midwinter; in fact it is all wealth, though it resembles the meanest poverty. Branching off Main Street at right angles, up small hills and down gentle slopes, the other streets: short but spacious avenues, noble trees over the snowbanks, lawns under them. Actually it is one lawn, there being no hedges or fences or walls (during the burning summers, no privacy). The houses are variations on one house, a sort of palatial cottage; principally wood, you can see into most of them and through some, and they do not seem to rest solidly on the ground; the difference between them and a tent is precisely that between moving every generation and moving every month ...

Where the houses leave off lugubrious poetry begins: never-painted landscape, chiaroscuro of twigs and snow. Framed by a puerile architecture, a patchwork of advertisements, a frieze of restless and almost beautiful men and women. The country, there it lies, a fitful and mysterious source—nothing more. The source of the sunrises, the bad weather, and the food, and of certain books already a little out of date. For the country, in the old sense of the word, has ceased to exist. Wisconsin farmers are no longer rustics; they have become provincials. The former ardent, hungry, tongue-tied life with its mingling of Greek tragedy and idyll has come to an end. Labor for the men, labor-pains for the women, elementary passions like gusts of storm moving unembarrassed in empty hearts, strong minds empty from birth until death of everything but the images of fowls in the rain, lonesome barns in the yellow sunshine—all over and done with. Now, by telephones, the radio, and automobiles, the farms have been turned into a sort of spacious, uncrystallized suburb around towns like Claron; and between the town and the suburb the contact is close. Now hired men, for example, have the privilege of being in love with Miss Garbo, whose troubling face I find on a bright poster.

Here are the humble-looking churches, half of whose faithful are farmers; many variations, both in appearance and in doctrine, on one church. I attend an elaborate pageant of the Nativity. All of the congregation's tapestries and many of its best bed-sheets; rented crowns and curtains, silly angels painted on a backdrop of sky; footlights and spotlights worthy of an assembly of radio fans. A gaunt little girl in gilt and muslin represents the Angel of History; she plays theatrically, has a very modern body and a cropped honey-colored head, and even her solemnity suggests profane shows in the East. Other all too Western muses. An adolescent chokes on his words, as indeed the original shepherd probably did. One of the Wise Men has forgotten to take off his horn-rimmed spectacles. The Babe in the manger is electricity, which is moving and seems true. It is all moving and true. But as the collection-boxes on long handles are passed, rather too plaintive an appeal for generosity is made; one would suppose that there were niggardly church-goers. And a kindly deacon improvises this prayer:

"Dear Father, we thank Thee that we live in a day when men are given to enjoy many things that they never had before. Especially women—I think women's lives have been made easy and lifted out of the darkness, thanks to the right interpretation of Thy Scriptures. And dear Father, we hear at present a great deal of talk against

Thy church. It has its limitations, we know, but it has done a wonderful work for mankind. And what have they found to take its place? Until another institution comes along which can do that work better, let us be faithful to it. Bless us in the name of the Son who, as we have seen, was born unto us this day. Amen." I realize that it is not blasphemous, for it is only rhetorically addressed to God, not meant to be heard in heaven but overheard in this town. Thus the religion of Calvin, holding its own in society at all costs, is helping itself cease to be a religion at all, the little churches becoming—oh, let us say, clubs.

There is a denominational college. I imagine the president of a poor school as a solicitor, a beggar of bequests, moving with anxious sociability from deathbed to deathbed, an advertiser by word of mouth, a human form-letter, praising his institution and arousing pity for it at the same time. Scandal—an indecorous dance or sometimes any dance at all, an instructor whose opinions on any subject are foolhardy or whose private life is subject to any remark—may occasion an unpleasant talk with some elderly person who has already been generous, relatively generous, or even cause a will to be revised. He has another source of revenue to keep flowing: the tuition fees, which are high. The young people are lawless, effervescent with strong ideas, insidiously persuasive; if his puritanism is tyrannical or the curriculum behind the times, friendly fathers, impatient brothers, will let them go elsewhere or try to have him removed. It is an unhappy position; he must be nobly patient and politic... At all events, the college reflects some such mournful reasonableness, time-serving, and trembling.

There are fraternity houses. A black upright piano rather broken by jazz and loaded with sheets of it, a phonograph as large as a pulpit, a radio-set which resembles a diamond-shaped harp—these things at least represent an art, humbly. A shout up the staircase brings the "brothers" down, single file, like jurymen. Most of them are solid and rubicund, one or two slender ones with the dead-leaf complexion: men and large men at that, but they have the blushes, the look of haunted innocence of small boys. Handsome, as a group compared with other groups; the individual faces seem too fresh and too amiable. Republican principles, false-looking gestures of affection, more than one hand laid deliberately on the next shoulder, expert joking evidently meant to create an atmosphere of intimacy: these habits will be useful in later life if they are to be, for example, travelling salesmen or ward politicians. No sign of thoroughgoing candor; almost every speech is followed by an acute glance at someone, to see how it is being taken; each is playing up to the other. Uniformly young though of various ages, the embryo without any mature bias; not a single novice doctor or lawyer or journalist or mathematician; how are they going to choose their professions? They will have to follow their noses—nothing else here to follow. The chief work of the society, I learn, is to beat out of each other all conceit and incivility; what is exceptional passes for the former, what is undemocratic for the latter. The better part of genius, if any turned up here, would be discretion. Its chief amusement is the exchange of indecent anecdotes in half-official conclave; an aimless exchange, for watch is kept and any moral slackness, however lonely, punished with a sort of paddle. Apparently a boy who procured, for instance, an unexpurgated *Arabian Nights* could make his way through school by selling it page by page. But the paddle occupies a place of honor on a hook on the wall, under a photograph of the Venus de Milo. How, with this combination of mental saturnalia and friendly *auto-da-fé*, are they to learn even to choose wives? Choosing, as a human function, does not seem to be greatly favored…

And what of sensual pleasure (call it love) in this town? Out of sight, fraught with dangers up to a certain age, subject to ridicule or worse thereafter. Boyish passion, that of Daphnis and Cherubino alike—its joys are restricted to Latin countries; its pains flourish anywhere. Women who live alone, in these translucent houses, are easily chaperoned by their neighbors; most people never hear of adultery except when there is a murder trial; there are only one or two charmless loose women, who fulfil their destiny, furthermore, under a cloud of specific suspicions; which leaves, for the vicious or the exasperated, girls of the poorest families, hired girls: obscure nights in motor-cars which are like rudderless boats, a handful of touches, farewells charged with resentment, finally an unpleasant reputation among other men. Americans like what is public, feel cheated by what some other races especially enjoy, the illicit; they dislike obliging their relatives to defend them; they dislike danger. To the young man with ambition enough to matter, premature marriage is the worst of dangers. It means earning a living by whatever is at hand; beggars of jobs cannot experiment, ought not to be far-sighted or fastidious. It means Wisconsin forever, with never any wholesome dissipation of a thousand chimeras—travels, ambitions, curiosities. That illusions should come to grief is the first step toward contentment; early marriage keeps as many hopes as are left intact, embalms them in a safe irreality, and keeps the young husband too young at heart. And almost any girl may spring, under the feet of a beau who suits her, any sort of man-trap. In general the young men mind this danger as well as the others. But fright is a strong stimulant; after dark there is a vibrant atmosphere of pleasure—worried, adored, and left to its meager resources. Fever takes the wheel of the autos. In the round of sufficient amusements, a more or less alert suspicion of their sweethearts and themselves; they must keep their self-control, must keep their bodies safe and sound, must keep from proposing. Under the soft maples, nervous teasing and erotic songs whistled and shrubs jetting their moist flowers and a lump in every throat. Syncopated bewilderment on the dance-floors; the music melts their hands and knees, but nothing is any easier. In the motion-picture theaters, thanks to the disastrous and vacillating ease in Miss Garbo's face—more fever.

A modest theater, shaped like a garage; but it is the imagination's chapel in this town, the small temple dedicated to licentiousness, aspiration, ideals. On the brick wall, on easels on the sidewalk, samples of what it has to offer: the abnormally large and liquid eyes of a beauty; the ridicule and pity of ill-fitting shoes; distant crystal and iron seas; foreign luxury, fashion shows, garden parties white with diamonds and swans. Every plot is founded on restlessness

and good luck; every film is a documentary film, fantastic only in
relation to its subject—realistically true to the imaginations to
which it is addressed. There they all flock to see, not really a world
brought to their door, but themselves in every foreign and domestic
disguise; themselves as they might be, convincingly photographed
where they are not—the variable bodies of other Narcissuses on
other mesmerizing streams. And in the dark and pleasant silence,
unreasonable music smooths their troubled foreheads. What might
be a stimulant is another narcotic. Their restlessness is merely
played upon, to pass the time—played upon and just enough, from
day to day, appeased. Meanwhile the time does pass.

One would think of Wisconsin as the ideal state to live in, a
paragon of civic success, but for the fact that the young people
dream only of getting away. And there are already a fair number of
Middle-Westerners about the world; a sort of vagrant chosen race
like the Jews. It is our better luck to leave behind in our Palestine
a teeming, prospering family, to fall back on in case of disaster
and to save us, meanwhile, from the nervousness of vagabonds
who really have no native land left. But we are more than likely
to call New York, that palace-hotel, home; the midland gets little
glory and even less entertainment from our activities. A great
maternal source of, among other things, ability and brutal ardor
and ingenuity and imagination—scarcely revisited, abandoned,
almost unable to profit by its fruitfulness in men.

Upon these renegade children, voluntary exiles, adventurers and
emigrants, brothers, cousins, or acquaintances—the others, those
who have not yet taken flight, even those who never will, speculate
a great deal in their own interest. They envy our apparent moral
emancipation, our pocket money literal and otherwise, the gaiety
which, if nothing more, we bring home to show them. They dread
risks we seem to have run, suspect abnormalities which may have
abetted us. What they admire most is our good luck; we are the
favorites of chance, goddess whose mythology the films have spun.
They ask question after question and prefer not to take advice.
Most of them will remain what they are, where they are—reality

only a little poisoned by notions of themselves freed and perfected, of pleasanter societies and facile foreign cities.

For those who dare not go east to meet the future, there is the hope that it may little by little be coming to them. Dreading isolation, most of them keep in line in spite of any eagerness; they do regret that the Middle West is so slow to change, but there is no comfort in anything unless all act together. That Basque beret at which the two workmen in the train stared—my brother asks me not to wear it in the street; but having seen in a New York magazine widely circulated out here a recommendation of such headgear, I can assure him that he will have to buy one for himself presently. The same law applies to manners and morals. The peculiar juvenile debauchery which in the East resulted from prohibition, that very Western law, has already crept westward; aided by drink, certain young married sets have begun to make the simplest experiments in immorality; every irregular problem ever thought of may well be on its way.

By birth the best of these young people are Protestants of some sort; by accident, or thanks to their own efforts, the classic Protestant rules have given way to an almost equally scrupulous open-mindedness. The doctrine of their elders imposes on them a certain lack of candor; they are wonderfully adroit; the danger is that in an admirable maze of diplomacy, discretion, and amiability they may lose track of their impulses. They are eminently reasonable, and wish neither to be hampered by old nonsense laid down as law nor to be exposed to the least persecution, but to be informed about the consequences of daring which is greater than their own; so that when the time comes they need not court disaster in the way that others have done. Individually they have few fundamental prejudices; the intolerance of Western society as a whole now seems to rest upon timidity about talking to each other. Their heresies are all hypothetical and they are in a certain sense courtiers, perfectly willing to compromise, to manoeuvre, to turn about as the wind blows, and meanwhile to do the greater part of their experimenting in imagination or vicariously.

Hence their enthusiastic appetite for a certain type of very rare fiction in which, in so far as the author has them, the key to personal liberty, the ledgers of genuine revolutions, shall be given. A literature of fresh convictions and agility in avoiding sorrow, of caprice, intoxications, and tenderness without shame; offering—to the new generation on stock-farms, in suburbs and sleepy colleges—the advantages of travel, the advantages of recklessness at a distance and vicarious trial flights; unexpurgated reports from the laboratories in which the future of conduct, their conduct, is being experimented upon; some tart breath of the sumptuous though menaced time to come; some sort of *Chanson de Geste* to provoke and ravish this imaginative soldiery to violent effort, to an intelligent looting of liberties, to a final ripe and amused peace … They do ask for a certain cheerfulness; one cannot expect those who seek the future in literature to wish to be altogether discouraged. I have not hitherto believed that the search for the future in literature often leads to good literature; be that as it may. No more weather-bound farmers, they beg; no more of the inarticulate, no more love limited to unfortunate stables and desperation growing faint between rows of spoiled corn, no more poverty-stricken purity, no more jeering or complaining about lamentable small towns … They or their fathers have had enough of all this. Who can blame them?

I at least do not, as in my mother's spare room I try to put in final order the manuscript of the book of which this diary, this stock-taking, is to form a part, and which scarcely seems inspiring or prophetic. It is no eagle for these ambitious, often heavy-hearted Ganymedes. Nor can it be very instructive: how could I expect natives of Wisconsin to see in the first story in the collection or the last my comment on, let us say, their flight or desire to fly to such questionable utopias as New York and Montparnasse?

It does represent, the whole collection, be it Wisconsin's fault or my own, a strangely limited moral order. Drunkenness; old or young initiations into love; homesickness in one's father's home for one's own, wherever it may be, or the more usual sort with its attendant disappointment; the fear of God; more drunkenness.

Roads and piazzas and lawns (always out of the corner of one's eye the haunting landscape, the haunted sky, the brindled fields, the four seasons with their over-ornate weather), small houses and small towns and other tiresome roads. That is all there is to it. And set beside a complicatedly unfolding reality, it seems little or not enough: too formal, as one's view of something which in one's childhood one did not expect to see change; now too squalid and now too noble; painted with too rudimentary a rainbow.

Then, with a sense of an immortal task and a mortal weariness, it comes time to return to New York, which is halfway back to the south of France. How much sweeter to come and go than to stay; that by way of judgment upon Wisconsin. The dark red railway station reminds me of Germany, the dim country into which the polished tracks lead away, of Russia—that is, of a place I have never seen. The orchards on the horizon look like black crêpe; there is a little lacquer sunset; useless and uselessly somber things, vainglory of God. Just as a child finds omens all about, I feel glad that I have never written a line for which there is any earthly use. Above the sunset the evening star blazes away superfluously, Mars or Venus in a sky composed of frost—though there is fighting only once a lifetime and, I suppose, less love-making than anywhere else in the world…

The train scarcely leaves the dim roofs and yellow windows behind before I feel my imagination beginning to be drawn away elsewhere, to several places irrelevant to each other at once; it is as if half the world were made of magnets. I fight against these charms and suspiciously close Gide's *Les Nourritures Terrestres*, which I had begun to read; my life of the rest of the year will get under way all too soon. Two young women across the aisle try to discover what my book is; theirs is a novel about Helen of Troy. They are workingwomen; I know because I hear them talking about a raise of their wages; but they are as arrogant and delicate as if they were kept. At present the West is a women's world; their bright minds make up its heart. But men's hearts suffer, in 1927, a strangely intellectual ferment…

I change trains, and throbbing on the rails the engine climbs up toward the town called Marblehead, which starts the same train of thought as before. It is the Greeks and Romans and the traditions preserved in Europe by the translators of Plutarch and by Montaigne and Goethe which, if one is an American, exasperate the imagination. Traditions of the conduct of life with death in mind… Few Americans are reasonable enough even to demand of seventy years their entire sweetness; the fame of too few will outlast, anywhere except in heaven, their mortal bodies. For various reasons we are, in 1927, the dominant nation in the world; there are, nevertheless, in 1927, more Frenchmen than Americans whose lives are to be memorable. (For Lindbergh and Isadora Duncan God be praised…) But I believe that American youngsters are equal in force, elasticity, beauty, and other natural gifts to the Greeks. In the fourth university year, let us say; not much longer. Something happens to them; the flower turns out to be seedless. Now all the causes, the mysterious stamens, are undergoing subtle transformations, perhaps for the better, perhaps not. It is a grave situation; and I believe that in the near future descriptive writing about average American destinies must inevitably be that of a reporter, an analyst, a diagnostician.

What may be called honest portrayal of a period of transition, of spiritual circumstances changing for an entire race, requires a fastidious realism, minute notation of events in their exact order, and the special sobriety of doctors or of witnesses at a trial. The more such an author has in common with his characters the better; typical trivialities surpass in significance the noblest feelings; an immediate report is more valuable than reminiscences. The rest is lyricism: the hero's shameless ode in praise of his own fortune or, even in the great, dim, half-attentive courtyard of the Mississippi Valley, a sort of serenade…

For fiction may combine in various proportions poetry and journalism. Poetry dispenses with chronology; it offers object or emotion as an end in itself during one moment which is assumed to be eternal, or under conditions as unfluctuating as those of the golden age; it must have some sort of immutability as a foundation. So I decide that the novelist who is or wishes to be anything of a poet will avoid such problems as, for example, Wisconsin is now likely to suggest; and will try to contribute to the appetites which make themselves felt there rather than to portray the confusion in which they arise. And no judicious novelist, however prosaic, will strive to outdistance life; he will choose problems which only seem insoluble, which in some corner of society, on some small illustrative scale, have been solved. The future of American civilization is a genuine riddle. The riddle of a sphinx with the perfect face of a movie star, with a dead-leaf complexion which is the result of this climate, our heating system, our habits…

Over many little bridges the train makes a soft thunder. A piece of moon has come up. In front of it a grove of naked trees, a flat expanse of dreary silver tarnished by weed-tops thrusting through it, a broken-looking house, a town, a living but icy river, rapidly give place to each other; as in the foreground of a writer's attention possible subjects for a book vary and shift before that waxing, waning, one-sided radiance which is his own spirit and about which alone he has no choice.

An English friend of mine once took to visit her father in the country a young American painter of some note. A year or two later he had an exhibition in Paris; she told the aging gentleman about it and asked if he remembered the American. "Ah yes, yes. That was the young man who didn't know where he was born. I thought it very curious."

"Now what made you think that, father? You misunderstood. He was born in the Middle West."

"But that's just it! I asked him, and that is precisely what he said—all he could tell me."

That, I believe, is a parable. A place which has no fixed boundaries, no particular history; inhabited by no one race; always exhausted by its rich output of food, men, and manufactured articles; loyal to none of its many creeds, prohibitions, fads, hypocrisies; now letting itself be governed, now ungovernable…

The Middle West is nowhere; an abstract nowhere. However earnestly writers proud of being natives of it may endeavor to give it form and character, it remains out of focus, amorphous, and a mystery. And by attempting to be specific as in these notes of my visit I have done, one over-particularizes, inevitably. What seems local is national, what seems national is universal, what seems Middle-Western is in the commonest way human. And yet—there is the sluggish emotional atmosphere, the suavity of its tedium, the morbid grandeur of its meanest predicaments; or are these illusions of those who take flight, who return? There is no Middle West. It is a certain climate, a certain landscape; and beyond that, a state of mind of people born where they do not like to live. A certain landscape? All the landscapes, except the noblest: the desert, the alp, the giant seas. One of its climates, one of its anarchic aspects clings to every memory, and deforms or charges with excessive lyricism the plain facts; so the winter, dazzling and boring as it is, has brooded too much over this account. There are other aspects, other seasons. In recent years I have not been at home except in midwinter or midsummer; next time I shall try to come in the fall…

A season which cannot be nationalized; wherever there are carts of gathered food, rumpled skirts, laborers, there is Brueghel. Overhead, the gray and blue of the iris of an eye, a calm clear gaze now animated by sensitive winds, now short-sighted with raindrops. The season of the eye, of supreme decoration: maroon with gun-metal, canary-yellow with silver, mahogany with pewter. About sundown farm-hands sing—what matter whose songs? The five senses saying goodbye; a whisper in the girls' ears, "Next summer we'll do it again." Out of the rags of husk comes the necessary corn; the hands, hard and flushed, wear beaks of steel for this work. Tobacco, butternuts, apples, and bitter grapes—the mouth is keen because it is getting cold. Harvest is the second or third oldest human contentment. It is never great enough, fortunately. Perennial disappointment to keep hope alive; so one is carried on from year to year. The last sunshine of every year is as bright as a wasp.

Perhaps I should enjoy myself more in the spring. There can be no disappointment then, for one expects nothing but promises and illusions. Sorrow is merely desire and all the joy promiscuous. Hepaticas under the rags of snow, blood-root, arbutus, and deadly nightshade, violets, mandrake, famished-looking lilies, iris, and cinnamon roses. Fruit trees: first, bony branches with negro skin and in due time their metamorphosis—angels' flesh, soft, mauve, milky, scented, roseate. In the sky other multiple branches, trailing vines, and wet sunken shadows: a colorless Everglades of cloud. The grass is like a sponge dipped in vinegar and perfume. Persian lilacs lay wreaths on the girls' shoulders as they pass in the lanes. Even the funerals are ragged with wild garlands; even the dead marry the ground; even the weddings sparkle with tears of rain. Rainbows and a profusion of birds. A wedding profusion of strange flowers, from the breast to the thighs of Wisconsin a rain of bouquet...

I realize that there are also mediocrities and spavined horses and tuberculous men, misery and streaks of madness, just as there were on the last farms before automobiles and electricity; but my mind leaves them out. One thing is certain: Wisconsin is no longer a wilderness. But I now know that a garden is better than any wilderness. Men and women have human stature in it and feel a greater number of satisfactions and disappointments; there is less cruelty, less involuntary cruelty at least.

I should like to write a book about ideal people under ideal circumstances. No sort of under-nourishment, no under-education, nothing partial or frustrated, no need of variety or luxury—in short, no lack of anything which, according to its children, Wisconsin denies. Only the inavertible troubles, all in the spirit, and only those characteristic of a period in which, here and there, certain bans have been lifted, certain jealousies appeased. The ease of mature and healthy plants in a well-kept garden, but an indoor book, in which human beings alone, not the weather or swamps or the beasts of the field, shall have parts to play. I am content that it shall pass for tragedy; even the arias of Mozart, the love-making of Daphnis and Chloe, hurt. And when that is done,

I shall have to ask myself whether, like Emerson and Whitman, I lack the vision of evil …

A little Italian brakeman, hurrying through the train, shouts, "Milwau-kee! Milwau-kee!" giving back to the syllables their red-Indian sound. I have some time before a train goes on to Chicago and climb up into the little park beside the station. Snowy bluffs over the fresh-water sea. On the other side of the real sea I shall miss this exciting air, which is to make a new race of us if nothing else does. Indeed it is melancholy leaving this land in which democracy is coming to a climax, in which a whole uneven generation is beginning to claim as its right, not merely the rewards, but the powers of supermen. The moonlight is brilliant because the windows of the thick-set Germanic buildings are not too close, because of the ice drifting on the water or attached to the shore. The bluish stars have horns. There are no boats in the harbor.

Then, wishing like Gide in his youth "to have been born in a time when, to celebrate all things, the poet had only to enumerate them," I remember the ports which seem to me more beautiful than this: the Hudson River whose lowing steamships send into your sleep flocks of great marine cattle; the Pool of London, a hollow and perhaps criminal cave under the fog of amber; the port of Marseilles shaped like a drinking bowl, wreathed with nets and rigging, and giving off an odor of poison in spite of the dates, sea-chestnuts, sea-potatoes, lemons and olives; the bay of Naples over which, on roofs, balconies, and perilous streets like tree-branches, figures out of the *comedia del arte,* beaked, ragged, clear-eyed as birds, gesticulate and play evil tricks and sing; and the roadstead of Villefranche. The latter lies in a broken ring of dim olive-trees; and between the lemon-white quay and the battleships, sailors signal to each other with an alphabet of outstretched arms and small flags like handkerchiefs on sticks, their faces gone blank with concentration. For another book I should like to learn to write in a style like those gestures: without slang, with precise equivalents instead of idioms, a style of rapid grace for the eye rather than sonority for the ear, in accordance with the ebb and flow of sensation rather than with intellectual habits, and out of which myself, with my origins and my prejudices and my Wisconsin, will seem to have disappeared.

The Runaways

II.

The Runaways

The sky rolled from side to side like an animal in pain, outstretched on the soft, saturated trees. Now and again there was a groan of thunder, and lightning played with a glitter of enormous eyes rolling in their sockets.

The lamp in the cross-roads saloon hollowed out a space in the darkness into which the rain poured, in which it was as bright as tin. Charlie Fox knelt there in the mud and admired this brightness. Then, dreamily, he set out toward home—to be more exact, toward the pleasant sour fragrance of the vegetation half-floating, half-rooted, in the fields. He could not endure bad weather unless he was drunk, when it meant nothing to him. He lay in the mud, lurched into cold creeks, stumbled through the underbrush at the side of the road, blustered and hiccoughed, collapsed backwards into a ditch or the flooded grass. His obstinate sighs mixed with the wind as it pulled the clouds away. He always got home safely at last. His daughter Amelia left a lamp rolled low in a window to guide him to his bed, but he usually tumbled quietly into the haymow.

The eighty-acre farm which he had inherited was a miserable thing to be dependent upon. Gashed with gullies, the fields of red clay sloped acutely toward the house and barn, which were half hidden in the edge of a swamp. In the center of this swamp, like an immense ditch, lay a lake into which the rains kept carrying the top-soil. Charlie Fox's father, understanding the farm's weaknesses, had kept the upper acres in sod-crops, filled the gullies with stone, planted clover to nourish the soil, rotted the straw in the barnyard, and hauled it with manure into all the fields in turn. In his youth Charlie had learned these hard lessons, but preferred to forget them. He planted only a little oats for the horse, a little corn for the cattle. The fences tottered and fell under the loads of woodbine and wild grapes. In large pastures full of thistles two or three sharp-hipped cows gnawed the June-grass that grew between the stones.

Charlie hired out by the day to his neighbors. They liked him, remembering his good nature whenever his bad habit made him a nuisance. One autumn, for example, having wandered away too frequently to a bottle behind a beam in the wagon-shed, he had dropped his pitchfork into a threshing machine, spoiling the blades which cut the twine; the owner had cursed and threatened, but in the end Charlie was not even obliged to pay for the damage. He was satisfied with this way of life—moving irresponsibly from farm to farm, working in no hurry, spending his earnings on drink when the weather was bad, his spare time mooning about the countryside. The roads were white, and pointed into distant hollows and distant forests, or lifted up to pierce the sky: arrows pointing to the sickly solitude that he loved…

His wife and daughter lived like a pair of domestic animals in a pen: coarse trees on three sides, one of Charlie's roads on the other, no variety, no entertainment, no plans, nothing to expect but that poverty would pinch them more and more cruelly; and they were bound to this man who was happy in a mysterious way, and so did not care.

As a tall wry-faced girl, Mrs. Fox, having been assured by her brothers that she need not expect to be courted for her looks, had married Charlie to avoid becoming an old maid. Charlie's mother had suggested that he might wake up and get his feet on the ground when he married; his bride had taken the chance and lost.

"Everything's goin' to pieces," she complained. "It's the worst-lookin' place in the county. Look at that broke rig with the weeds growin' through the wheels. The tools all out gettin' rusted. I'll be switched if even the mare don't look mangy!"

"Oh, stop it, Ma!" Amelia grumbled. "What good does that kind'a talk do?"

"Nobody goes by on the road," her mother went on, "nothin' to see, nothin' to do. And me sick. Your pa gets the best of it, he gets out among folks. We women don't get no further'n you could throw a stone."

Amelia marched across from the sink, her round shoulders raised, shaking her dishtowel angrily. "Who's to blame for this God-awful marsh? What's the use'a so much whimpering? Who's to blame, I ast you? Better lie down, Ma, and rest."

As soon as the girl went out to do the milking the sick woman shuffled away to bed. If it rained she tossed back and forth among the quilts and pillows, kept awake by the water which streamed in all the gullies, washing the best of their land down to the lake, temporary rivers with an echo in the universe, gurgling and growing thick, without foam. Soon there would be nothing left but rocks like a lot of skulls between the fences.

Amelia was a short, displeasing, muscular girl. Her chapped skin seemed to have been drawn tight over the bones of her face — over the long nose, the not quite symmetrical cheek-bones, the stubborn receding chin — drawn tight and fastened in back by her knotted hair. When she did not pout, her lips were scarcely to be seen.

She did all the chores as well as the housework: gave the cattle frozen corn-fodder to supplement the straw which they ate from the stack, milked them and took the can to the cheese factory, pumped from the stinking vat her share of whey for the pigs. Down trenches which she had shovelled in the snow-drifts she staggered with slopping pails of swill, her long arms almost pulled from their sockets. At butchering time she worked elbow to elbow with the men, scraping the bristles from the carcasses soused in boiling water; and she alone cut up the pork, rubbed and smoked the bacon, ground the sausage meat and stuffed the intestines with it. On spring nights she watched for hours over the old sows while they farrowed, lest they eat their young. Her last duty was to turn down the lamp in the window which her father could see as he stumbled up the road.

The lake in the swamp contained black bass and pickerel. It belonged to a paralytic widow in Milwaukee; so Charlie posed as its proprietor and rented his flat-bottomed boat to fishermen two or three times a week, which seemed to him an ideal source of revenue. One Sunday morning a young man named Nick Richter drove up before the barn with two bamboo poles wagging behind his buggy, and Amelia showed him where to tie his horse and brought the heavy oars from the shed.

He soon became Amelia's suitor. His father had been a blacksmith; just before he died, having speculated in Texas oil, he had been forced to sell his house, his shop, and every hammer and horseshoe in it. Nick had no home, but worked here and there, chiefly in the towns, at odd jobs. He bought a horse and buggy when he could afford to, and sold them when he was out of work; and at every Saturday and Sunday night dance for years tried to make a good marriage. But he danced with his jaw, his neck, and his elbows; the boisterous girls merely laughed at him. These entertainments were also expensive; he grew discouraged. Having found Amelia, he had only to take her to the lake to fish or pretend to fish, and could save a little money.

A fragrant old road led down through the swamp. Near the lake the water glimmered between the boughs in mother-of-pearl strips. Over it and over the treetops murky hills lifted their feeble, capricious beauty. A muddy channel led from the tottering boathouse out through the reeds to a cup-shaped harbor, separated from the deep water by a sand bar. In this quiet place a few lilies grew, the yellow variety thrusting above the surface its hard serpent heads, the white spreading out tufts of morbid plumage. Here the boat was at rest, the oars hanging from the oarlocks. Along the shore autumn leaves, dead bodies of leaves, shadows of leaves, fell and floated among the water-lilies. Nick crouched in the bottom of the boat, half-hidden, and Amelia, sitting on the broad back seat, held his head on her lap in her hands. There was a wan, stupid look of ecstasy on her face, an ecstasy of possession without confidence that she could keep him, without hope that she would be any better off if she did.

One morning that fall when an odor, iced and musky, came out of the forest and the dewy red leaves looked swollen, the thickets very large with mist, Amelia went into the barn soon after daybreak. Light came in, a feeble quivering of it, from the two peepholes and innumerable cracks. The loud sparrows were up and about. Amelia first saw a pair of heavy boots, smeared with dry mud, the toes turned sharply outward, and beyond them and between them Charlie's face, tough, snow-white, and disdainful, hay in his hair and several stalks in his mustache. She shook him and found that he was dead.

Then Amelia was sort of heiress; the man who married her would have a farm of his own. Nick married her at once.

Her dying mother expressed gratification, rather peevishly. "Amelia couldn't stand it, bein' alone. I ain't much company no more." She grew steadily weaker, and kept the young bride at her bedside all that winter, reproachful and insistent with her eyes when she could not speak. They buried her in April.

"Of course I'll miss her, and she was always good to me," Amelia kept saying at the funeral, as if to come up to someone's expectations, hiding her eyes in a clean handkerchief.

Someone asked, "Are you and Nick going to stay on the farm?"

"I don't know."

"I thought you might try something else. The land isn't much good, is it?"

"Good for nothin'," she said. "Nick's plumb disgusted. He says I ought to've told him. But I was sweet on him. Oh Lord! that land's wore out, sandy — stone and ditches. It's gettin' now so's it won't raise grass — never was manured any. And the fences are all down. God! I hate it!

"Well, not just because it's poor farmin'. I don't know — the woods maybe, those rotten trees so close. It's no way to live; you see 'em all day and hear 'em all night. When I was a kid I used to be scared our house would slide into the lake. Was you ever down there? It just shows you what it's always been like. If you fell in, you'd have some chance. But if you was always in ..."

Her voice became a wild whisper. "You need some excitement. I never went nowhere, never saw nothin'—had to work. I guess you wouldn't have the nerve to get out of a dead hole like that if you knew you got to come back. That's why I never went to dances. I guess you'd jump into the lake for good—when you got home, I mean."

"Why don't you sell the whole outfit and rent a house near town?" someone asked. "Nick could make as much in town by the day as he does here."

She did not seem to be listening. "And it's so awful still," she muttered. "My God! It's so still you can hear the slime dripping in the well."

"Sell it and go to town. Nick could make two or three dollars a day. Don't try to stick it out another year. Give yourself a chance. Have an auction."

"What?" she cried. "Sell that junk? Lord, it wouldn't bring thirty cents. Spread all that rubbish round the yard for a lot of old women to pick over? I should say not. Oh, I couldn't," she lamented. "I couldn't go off and leave the house, everything the way it's always been. It'd be like leaving one'a them, Ma or Pa—like not burying them," she said.

That spring Nick put in only the patch of oats for the horse, ploughed up the garden for Amelia, and began to hire out to his neighbors as Charlie had done. He was a good worker in his sour, muttering way, but he was not popular. Holding out his red wrists stiffly was all that he ever did to show willingness. He was bad-tempered, and growing worse every day. Perhaps his marriage was a disappointment; without doubt, in so far as he had been able to imagine such things, he must have missed the serenity of a married man, the security of a man of property. How could he have helped being contaminated by Amelia's reckless discontent? Perhaps he was afraid of her: a weak swimmer who had ventured into what looked like a stagnant pool, to find himself in the embrace of a profound, indomitable current…

By autumn she had brought him around to her point of view—less a point of view than a mania, a waking dream. She would stand a long time under the poplars full of blackbirds, glaring at the exhausted soil gaping through the grass, the thin stand of grain, the capacious parched gullies, the trees asleep in the sunshine. Then she would shout raucously and chase the hens around the yard with a stick. Every day she killed one and they ate it, until they were all gone.

"There ain't no sale for such a place," Nick told her. "Your pa had it insured for more'n it was worth—he didn't know no better."

In consequence, she got out the insurance policy and pored over it by the hour; it was hard for her to read; but there at the head of the page it said five thousand dollars—that was hers, the company had no right to keep it, she would have it.

One morning they packed a small tin trunk, put it under the buggy seat, and covered it with a horse-blanket. They had sold the cattle, but they had to leave the hogs behind. Nick had brought home a bottle in honor of the occasion, and took a drink to give him courage. Then they made a pile of newspapers and bed-quilts in the cellar, lit it, and drove away as fast as they could toward Belleville, taking indirect wooded roads lest they be turned back by someone who had heard the news.

In the semicircle of swampy forest the little house squatted, stared from its uncurtained windows which resembled idiot eyes without eyelashes. The sheds leaned against the barn. A sick dove staggered over the rocks by the water-trough. A little way from the kitchen door some shirts, stockings, and torn dish-towels hung on a line stretched between two posts; Amelia had said, smiling from ear to ear, "Leave them things there, so's the neighbors won't think any harm." Indoors the breakfast dishes lay in and around a dishpan of cold water, and the fire in the range was only a handful of pink coals; but one could have smelled smoke, and finally it began to curl up through the cracks in the floor.

Down the road a fat man named Beacon sat on his lawn, a pitcher of water beside him, fanning his wet face with a newspaper. In hot weather, on account of his weight, he had to leave the hard work to his sons. He beckoned to a passer-by and went down, wheezing and ponderous, to the road. "Hey, as you went by Fox's," he asked, "did you see anything of Nick?"

He was deaf, so his neighbor shouted. "Nobody there. I wanted to get him myself, so I stopped by their house."

"Whew!" the heavy man sighed. "Nobody there. Queer. Nick's been helpin' us out, and he hain't showed up today. He al'ays sends word. I thought he must'a been sick."

"Now that is funny. Amelia wasn't there, neither."

"Well, it's a new wrinkle for Nick," Beacon concluded mournfully.

At the Hope's Corner store someone noticed a faint smokiness in the air. Someone else said, "It comes down from the forest fires in the north of the state."

A vast black mushroom rose over the swamp. When the wind broke it up, the smoke, thick and steady and the color of wheat chaff, rolled slowly overhead.

Through a hole in the roof a great draught lifted the flame as if in a chimney. The yard filled with men, their faces in the ruddy light spectral and glistening. They fought the fire eagerly and with some skill. They chopped down the flaming porch. Sweat dripped under their blue shirts. Three of them in turn working the handle of the coughing, spurting pump, and bucket after bucket of water was passed from hand to hand and emptied.

A good many buggies, wagons, and autos drew up along the road; several women looked on with interest, their summer dresses and parasols lending to the catastrophe an air of picnic. Among the spectators but near enough to make his advice heard above the crackle and roar of the fire, the other shouts, the axes, the creak of the pump-handle, old Beacon was enthroned on a dry-goods box. "Well," he demanded, between orders, "what d'you think of this? They had it insured." He winked. "Well, I'll be damned, anyhow." He swelled out his cheeks and blew wearily.

The roof fell, splitting like paper, and after that the fire diminished. The floor sent up smoke and steam, but no more flame. The kitchen stove crashed through the charred boards into the cellar.

"But I don't know what these men are burstin' themselves for, at a job like this," old Beacon said. "Looks to me like nobody's goin' to thank 'em for it. The mare and the cart're gone. An' everythin' else of any value, I'll bet."

The flames left a ruin shaped like a charred pot. The men drew off—wet, black, tired, and puzzled—washed their faces at the pump and rolled down their sleeves. The horses were untied, everyone piled into one vehicle or another, and they drove away shouting; but those who spoke of the cause of the fire did so in pairs, very quietly.

From the foul and broken house the smoke went up straight to the sky. Now it was soft as wool, now like a shell or a tower of shell. It widened over the swamp, casting a shadow on the lake, and persisted until dusk with an even melancholy trembling.

Meanwhile over the little wooded hills Nick and Amelia were in flight, though they did not realize it at first, having intended to drive back toward evening, to hide their trunk in a gully, and pretend to be heartbroken. Nick had brought his bottle along; he was not used to drinking, so he giggled like a small girl and amused himself by picking the brightest leaves from the trees as they passed. Amelia drove. Suddenly she began to whip the horse. "I'm not goin' to stop at Belleville," she said. "I'm going to Fond du Lac; it's a big place."

"We've got to go back home and put in the claim for the insurance, you blamed fool."

"I won't. I tell you I won't. I don' want to. We can get the money in Fond du Lac." She whimpered and looked over her shoulder.

"What's the matter with you, anyway? Are you afraid of the fire? Are you ashamed of yourself? You ought to be." He slapped her, but that did not prevent her from turning down a road which led toward the larger town.

"Oh, I don't know, I don' care. But I'm not goin' back home any more. Lord! I hate that place. And you're supposed to work for old Beacon; he'll be awful mad and he'll make out who started the fire." Her hair had come down; her face was weary and yellow; her mouth twitched as if she were angry. She went on whipping the old mare.

Then, thanks to the bottle, Nick decided that she was funny, and took everything in good nature. They had nothing to eat all day. Toward sunset they arrived in Fond du Lac. Nick had worked there and knew his way about; Amelia had the money from the sale of the cows in her stocking; they took a room in a boarding-house. That night Nick went to see a disreputable lawyer whom he knew, told him the story, and gave him the insurance policy.

The next day the lawyer went to Hope's Corner. He found old Beacon on his lawn, wearing a wet bandana handkerchief instead of a hat. "I am an insurance lawyer. I want to make some inquiries about that fire."

"The less said about that the better," Beacon replied. "Whew!" He settled his damp cheeks in the folds of his neck. "A plain case of arson. But they cleared out and gave the whole show away. They ain't much better at lawbreakin' than anything else. Well, the old house is burned to the timbers. It serves poor old Charlie Fox right for insuring his farm for more'n it's worth. And for havin' a halfwitted girl."

When the lawyer got back to town and told the fugitives that he would not take up their claim, Amelia cursed the insurance company and accused him of fraud; Nick burst into tears and said it was her fault and beat her. Then they went down to dinner at the boarding-house table.

The shuttered dining room smelled like a potato-cellar. When the landlady trotted out of the kitchen and set down platters of meat in slabs as large as her hand and bowls of bitter turnips in milk, the regular boarders looked with wan faces at their plates and at one another. Nick and Amelia had no appetites on account of their misfortune.

On their way into town they had passed two belated vans of a tent carnival, the horses' fetlocks stirring up dust in clouds which settled on the faces of several men with cheeks full of tobacco and a hatchet-faced woman who lay on some rolls of canvas. There were two ladies from this company at the boarding-house. These two ate with the silent heartiness of women paid to do so in a show-window as an advertisement of something. Under mats of blondined hair fastened with rhinestone pins, their faces had an identical appearance of cheap china. Their hard eyes lay still amid soiled eyelashes; the spots of orange rouge were too close to their ears; their nails, cut in triangles, shone like celluloid. Grasping their knives and forks vigorously, their eyes unfocussed, their red mouths in motion, they consumed the fat meat to the last drop of gravy, the soggy pie to the last crumb.

Amelia gazed at these two with open-mouthed admiration; they were her ideal. After dinner they passed out handbills and she engaged one of them in conversation, telling how their house had burned down and a lawyer her husband had picked out had cheated them of their insurance. Meanwhile the other asked Nick to come upstairs to help her move a trunk. Nick came down red-faced and flattered; and all four of them made their way to the dance-hall park, between the river and the railroad tracks, where the carnival had pitched its tents.

Five great wagons and a mud-caked Ford were drawn up on the banks of an untidy stream. The horses grazed in an adjoining vacant lot, sweat dried in flakes on their backs, switching at the flies and never lifting their heads to look at the tumultuous camp, unfolded out of the loads they had drawn.

In the center, like a fat woman pirouetting, the merry-go-round revolved laboriously. The minute stallions with mincing legs outspread and foamless lips parted, the pair of crimson tigers drawing a chariot for those too timid or too large to go astride, and the sky-blue bears—the power which set them gradually rocking and circling came from a steam engine shaped like a short-necked bottle, whose whistle preceded the slapping and squeaking of the leather belts and the outburst of shrill tunes from the calliope when all the passengers, mostly children, had been hoisted and set upright in the saddles.

A crowd of untidy women and shouting boys filled the alley between the tents. The refreshment booth, a great umbrella of canvas over planks laid from barrel to barrel, did a brisk business in ice-cream cones, tepid drinks, sandwiches, and sausages. A young man whose hair hung down in shoestrings and a young woman with brown pouches beneath her eyes ran from side to side, calling, "What's yours?" and, "Don't push, pleeease," storing the nickels and dimes in a cash-register drawer which opened and shut with a grating noise.

Next to it stood a Hit the Nigger Baby establishment: a hierarchy of dolls, a pile of baseballs with which to knock them down, and a display of bad cigars, vases, felt pillow-covers, and ash-trays, for prizes. Though it was Saturday afternoon, few grown men were there to patronize it; for those who had worked all morning in that heat naturally preferred to lie on couches indoors, alone, with newspapers over their faces.

Through the crowd, like two small children, Nick and Amelia followed the theatrical ladies, toward whom sometimes heads were turned and fingers pointed, because they were so rouged and fashionable. Who could have told which was the proudest then, the country wife or her sullen and fickle husband? They left their new friends at the entrance to the show, "Gay Paree," promising to go in when it began.

The leaves of the maples, pockmarked and bleached by a common blight, loosened and glided through the windless air; the calliope played, the barkers grew hoarse, many babies cried. The two who had run away from the country forgot their unsuccessful fraud, forgot the swamp, their hopelessness, the future, and wandered up and down, too happy to enjoy any particular thing. Already Nick was trying to seem accustomed to it all, hunching his shoulders as he always did, in the manner of a bad-tempered bird of prey. Amelia walked with a loose light-footedness, gazing in every direction at once, like one who has just come to paradise.

Finally they returned to the boarding-house with the shameless dancers. The result was that they joined the carnival company before it left Fond du Lac, contributing the horse and buggy and what was left from the sale of their two cows as capital. At first Nick drove a van and Amelia cooked sausages and patties of ground meat on a black pan in the refreshment pavilion, taking the place of the brown-cheeked woman, who had fallen ill.

For years they travelled about Wisconsin and up and down the Mississippi in this company. Business was not good; business was never good, or never good enough. It was a hard life: shouting, luring, brow-beating, laughing, and singing; eating the poorest food, counting the smallest coins, packing the tents, frayed finery, nigger dolls, fangless rattlesnakes, and petrified Belgian babies; the boss and his wife going ahead in the Ford to rent the next park, the rest following slowly after the strong-smelling horses. Nick and Amelia, as well as the youngest Gaiety Queen and the newest freak, learned that romance is for those who see, never for those who do, and underpaid as a profession.

Floating overhead there was a picture on slack canvas of the dope fiend, a moon-colored young man with scaly, allegorical beasts nestling against his ribs. Under it hung posters of Jocko, the Baboon Man, who spoke the monkey language and ate raw meat, a snake-charmer among her serpents, which stood up in spirals as thick as trees, and the Fat Woman, a belted and corsetted featherbed, with oval fingers scarcely meeting across her chest. A nervous little man who looked as if he might at any moment burst into tears lectured the people. Inside, the pale young man murmured, "Cigarette smoking has made me what I am today," and the charmer crooned perfunctorily to her sick snakes; the tent reeked with his ether and her toilet water. When he was feeling well, Jocko, the Baboon Man, tore off the heads of squawking live hens with his teeth and sucked their blood.

There was always a crowd in front of the other tent, "Gay Paree," perhaps because of the free show before the performance. Three women and a negro came out on a platform like a large bench. The women's diaphanous slips, all beads and fringe, did not cover a row of pink and green legs, two of which were crooked and four fat. They gazed at the crowd with the solemnity of caged animals and with an air of concentration; it was not easy to look voluptuous on the couchless, cushionless boards. One of them pulled her blouse away from her body and peered avidly inside it. The negro who was standing sleepily beside them crouched at a given moment and began to pipe, drearily and loud, on a sort of flute. The women stiffened, their lips parted, the pupils of their eyes grew large and still. Three arms were lifted, and all their bodies throbbed, paused, throbbed again. Then each one curved her waist extremely, first to the right side, then to the left, and each seemed to spring upward and outward and relax like a bow from which an arrow has been shot. Three shrill cries and a tapping of the negro's foot marked the time.

During the dance Amelia came out of the tent behind the performers and sat down in the ticket booth. As she took out the roll of tickets like a pulley wheel and counted the change in a box, her small eyes drifted loftily from dull face to dull face: so many strangers, so many fools, so many tickets to be sold…

She had grown fat and looked like a female jack-in-the-box. Her narrow lips had been pressed together gradually by rectangular cheeks; there were deep crevices at her wrists; the sharp chin-bone was lost amid a succession of double chins, gathered into a tight necklace of amber beads. Her hair was mounted in a pompadour over a visible brown rat. Her purple velvet dress had worn leathery at the elbows. Nevertheless, the way she sat in her booth like an improvised pulpit, the fruits of experience in her face, the new masses of her body, did make one think in some way of progress and prosperity and joy.

Nick's appearance between the flaps, coattails first, as he argued with someone inside the tent, silenced the music and arrested the dancing. He turned around and began to harangue the onlookers and to shake his large fists, straining the frock-coat which was buttoned too tightly across his chest. His glance was still hurt and ominous, and there was still the suggestion of a curse in the tone of his voice; the carnival had not been his salvation. Amelia alone, soothed by movement and noise, gorged with excitement, was satisfied; and without looking at him seemed to be making fun of his angry hands, the furtive hope in his eyes, the mastiff jaw that would never dare to snap.

"You have here, ladies and gentlemen," he continued, smiling conventionally, "the flower of Oriental art. It is no singing and dancing for children. There are things about it they would not appreciate. All these famous performers have appeared in Paris. The French do not relish tame entertainments. They like it hot and strong. You have seen their free preliminary dance. It is only a sample of what they can do. The admission is ten cents. I advise you strongly to come in. The show starts in five minutes."

The women and the negro sauntered down the steps behind the flap. Nick disappeared. Amelia began to tear off tickets and make change, and presently she followed. All was well; for in the dusty grove were tents, the brass throats of the calliope opened again, and the whole small town throbbed with music.

Adolescence

III

Adolescence

In the attic bedroom of a large house at twilight two young-sters were trying to make up their minds about a masquerade party. Out of the stairway rose an agreeable odor of bath-towels and tobacco and face-powder, reminding the younger boy of his friend's brothers and fashionable mother, whom he admired but who often embarrassed him. He came from the country, and was sensuous and timid.

Carl, who was at home there, was the youngest of the four sons of one of three brothers who owned the flour-mill and several stores and a number of houses in the town. Philip had only his father and mother, and they were poor. They were respectively fifteen and thirteen years old.

Both were excited by the illicit cigarette which Carl was holding outside the dormer window. Past his friend's face, whose cynical expression was meant to reveal and in fact greatly exaggerated the effect of the smoke, Philip gazed down into the quiet though populous twilight, leaf-green and pink. The small town rose from the river-bed on a number of overlapping hills; heaped with branches and evening silhouettes, the light color of the buildings died down.

It was from the bulky yellow house under the elms that they had received an invitation to a fancy-dress party. A girl named Rita who went to school with them lived there; she was going to be fifteen years old. They could not make up their minds what disguises to adopt. Philip's imagination ran to lace curtains and borrowed jewelry, but it was Carl who said: "I'll tell you what. You dress up as a woman. I'll get my brother's glee club suit and wear a mustache. We're supposed to wear masks, anyway, and they won't know you and I'll say you're my cousin from Milwaukee. You'll make quite a pretty girl. Just for the fun of it. See what it's like."

The next afternoon they asked his cousins Lucy and Lois in the house next door to help them. These two lovely sisters lived with their aged stepmother and a maiden aunt. Men of their age at once unmarried and worth marrying almost never appeared on the scene of the small town; they were clairvoyant and knew what to expect; so in spite of their fresh bodies and liquid eyes they already had the serene manners of sisters of charity. They were working at a frock for someone else; eyelet embroidery and ribbons and batiste lay in disorder on the polished table.

As Carl explained what they wanted he leaned against the mantelpiece sturdily, in imitation of his elder brothers giving orders to indulgent women. "You'll find him a dress, won't you? You have a lot of old stuff in the cherry cupboard."

The young women were charmed by the plan. Though Philip wanted to keep even his unspoken requests within modest bounds, he could not keep his poor farmer-boy's gaze from the rich work-table: the blueprint patterns, the bolt of white cloth like a flattened pilaster, the chiselled pleats, the squares cut out—transparent marble of some fresh and incomplete and ethereal architecture into which a chilly bare body could slip as into a dwelling…

He came there again two days later to be tormented by one of the worst forms of fatigue, that of erect immobility touched by many nervous hands, pinched and patient, measured, turned about, discussed, labored over. They stood him on a stool by way of a pedestal. The sharp mouths of two pairs of scissors played about him, as well as a quiverful of pins both black and nickel-plated, often piercing to the skin. He was as happy and nervous as a young martyr.

The excitement of the sisters increased as they worked. Out of some bright old rags, pins, coral beads, and a boy—a farm boy at that—they were creating a woman's charm. It might have been a symbolical doll that they were dressing, to attract, by some rule of magic, out of the sluggish village to themselves, a multiple and passionate attention: rude young beaux dangerously troubled in the dim bowling alley, gray-haired lawyers and doctors stealing across the lawn with gifts, perfect husbands chosen finally after the most luxurious hesitations, coming there by appointment to carry them off... Their rather young faces of spinsters by accident grew still younger, the pure mouths and the pinched nostrils animated by laughter, imagination, sighs.

Disturbed by this hilarity in the decorous house, their old maiden aunt came to the head of the stairs and called down, "What is the matter?"

Even Carl, comparatively useless and at ease like a proprietor, regarded his cousins with a new interest and wondered at the indifference of his brothers who were old enough to fall in love with them. When they were silent and busy their mouths remained slightly open, as if the invisible forms of the tones of their voices stayed on their lips. Because of them he began to feel the approach of a certain excitement in the night before him: a tumult of masked girls, lawns resilient under fleeing and pursuing feet, games which would be only a pretext for taking almost painful kisses and for laughing at them once taken—the approach of a sweet disorder in which he was very likely to forget his less and less recognizable friend.

The work was done. The sisters and Carl led the bedizened youngster into another room to a tall mirror. He wore an old-rose satin dancing frock, and long kid gloves, and on his head a black velvet picture hat out of which there pressed against the nape of his neck and his temples one of the blond wigs which the maiden aunt had worn before she had felt obliged to change to gray, unpleasantly soft and audible, sweet with cologne-water. The full skirt had been tucked up behind so that it resembled the tumbled plumage of some lean, pink swan; and out of the square bodice rose his unfamiliar throat powdered and wound with coral.

"I declare, he is prettier than any girl in the village," Lucy cried.

But during the vigorous remodelling which the dress had received at the sisters' hands, the enervate satin had lost the last of its freshness; the worn ruffles and the pulled seams held together with a bedraggled tenacity; the fairy-tale pink was veined with mauve. Philip's extreme youth of a boy made a woman's maturity; and in the mirror his face had the frightened expression of a woman who feels that she is too gaudily, too youthfully dressed for her age.

Over his puckered sleeves the sisters, radiant and amused, were looking; and between their faces in the mirror Carl's face, which astonished him. How could Carl's appearance be changed by his metamorphosis—or was he merely seeing him with the eyes of the part he was dressed to play? Smaller than before, hardy and provocative, masculine to an enigmatic degree, smiling a humorless, drowsy smile… The disguised boy met the other's glance, and thinking himself the cause of the equivocal expression, blushed.

Lois and Lucy said wistfully, "Have a good time," and said goodbye.

Together the boys crossed the adjoining lawns toward Carl's home. Philip was anxious on all occasions; in this preposterous costume, if he went into the house, he was certain to be teased unmercifully by Carl's brother; so he resigned himself to going without any supper.

There was a great maple tree on the lawn, inside which, on the lower limbs, the brothers had built a platform. Carl threw his arms around his friend's rustling knees and lifted him as high as he could. Philip caught a branch and carefully pulled himself up into the hiding-place.

"If you were a girl you'd gather your skirts together," Carl said. Then he hurried indoors to dine and put on his evening clothes and false mustache.

The sun had set; there would be no moon that night, so it must have been the earth which filled the sky with overtones of foliage and with the pearls of its pale buildings and pale fields. Inside the tree everything was dim and still. The platform on which Philip sat was enclosed by the light-colored, slim, wayward pillars of the branches.

He could smell the food being served inside the house; that was the first penalty of his adventure; he began to feel that it would not be the last. Ants went up and down the branches of the tree; he kept watch that none should get into his flounces. This led him to try to feel his boy's body inside them; he shook himself from head to toe, and decided that wearing women's clothes was like being tucked into a luxurious, portable bed. A whalebone in the old corset hurt him and had to be pushed back into place.

He listened to bicycles going down the streets and the discords of the different kinds of bells all over the town. Then he heard something else, this time on the lawn below, and hunted for it through the foliage. It was Carl's eldest brother, admirable, somber, and hurried. Philip shrank out of sight.

He was too young to find anything worth thinking about under such abnormal circumstances; so he let his imagination drift heedlessly, forgetful both of the nonexistent cousin from Milwaukee whom he was supposed to represent and the gallant widow, desperately eager to please, in weakened frills, whom in fact he did resemble.

Carl came back and climbed up in the tree until it should be time to go to the party. He brought the hungry masquerader some sandwiches and a bottle of root-beer. He lit a match, for it was almost dark, a flickering light among the dark, flickering leaves; and each adding to the somewhat exalted notion he had of his own appearance the comical image of the other, they laughed a little. Then they sat quietly and talked.

In spite of the difference in their ages they had entered high school together the September before, Philip coming from the farm to do so. The boys Carl had grown up with had been greatly inclined to bully the new, somewhat effeminate, rustic boy; Carl had defended him. In return, by the usual frauds, Philip had lightened for him the burdens of getting an education. On this basis they had become inseparable companions.

Philip's gratitude for being championed was flattering. In a childish way he was eccentric, which contrasted well with his friend's ideal banality, and his unpopularity satisfied in his friend rudiments of jealousy. He lacked common sense and offered instead the poetry of being surprised and being excited in all his five senses by everything and easily hurt. On the whole, Carl enjoyed in him qualities that he would later enjoy in women.

Outside the tree the swallows wheeled up and down, chattering, in front of the evening star.

The girl to whose fifteenth birthday party they were going might not have invited the new boy from the country, had she not had a weakness for Carl ever since an intimate summer afternoon in a forest when they were children. She wished to flatter him by acknowledging his right to be followed wherever he went by his small protégé. Up in the tree Carl told Philip about that afternoon.

Philip, on the other hand, would not have had the courage to go, but for Carl's insistence and the promise of protection which it implied. The latter, a little boastful about his knowledge of the world, replied to every expression of curiosity on his friend's part by a recommendation of actual experience. Philip had often asked what happened at parties in the village.

Giving anxious attention to his false mustache, Carl smoked another forbidden cigarette.

For several years Philip had had a constant sense of growing up; it was less a sense than a sensation, as if he could actually feel cells expanding, new nerves winding like tendrils of a vine about certain muscles, bones hardening. Goodbye childhood; and his imagination, genuinely terror-stricken, crying to maturity—coming, coming, coming! Himself as a grown man looked forward to, cherished with vain anxiety, wondered about, feared and forecast in innumerable juvenile ways … Thus it was as a sort of Narcissus that he had been ready to bend selfishly, attentively, toward the mirror of the life of a somewhat older boy such as his friend. Desire for himself, his prospective self, was a large part of his affection.

His friend's house poured out upon the grass a brilliant light, but it was almost silent. Only the nurse, hopelessly in love, was singing Carl's little sister to sleep with a lullaby in which there were panting tones that Philip did not understand.

He was miserably innocent, or believed himself to be, imagining, as adolescents do, that there is more to know than there is. Up on the platform in the maple tree, in the attitude of Narcissus over the pool of darkness and grass, almost flat on his stomach in spite of his finery, he asked Carl questions about girls, hoping for answers about men — that is, about himself. Carl replied in a shrouded, muttering voice, taking advantage of his own excitement, dealing roughly with his own modesty. The questions and the answers did not quite match; one imagined that he was preparing for life, the other was getting ready to have a good time at the party …

Then, here and there in the town, the hour of the party struck, and they went. It was not far. Rita's house reached through the trees to meet them with its arms of light lying loose and open on the grass, its cries of rough amusement made by many young guests. They put on their two small black masks.

A dozen or more dressed-up youngsters had arrived before them, as they had hoped. Carl got through the false introduction well enough, made very polite by the danger of laughing. Philip slipped into a chair which stood by itself in one corner.

In the rather rich rooms, untidy with imitation flowers and twisted streamers, red with paper lamp-shades, there were tramps who had tin boxes of hay-leaves for tobacco, Indian chiefs thrust full of rooster feathers, a soldier in the uniform of no particular country, two girls in wall-paper, a Fairy Soap girl carrying a bunch of millinery violets, a pallid dark-haired Irish girl as an Oriental dancer. These disguises were all the prettier for being hasty and imperfect, but there would be little left of them by midnight.

Philip should have received the prize for the finest costume, if there had been one, and did receive a great deal of sidelong scrutiny. Then the games began, which he was not asked to join, and with the games the rude flirtations.

A lamp shone in his eyes, but he preferred not to move. He was too young ever to have been so lonesome before. He could not make up his mind whether the other guests had recognized him. They had not done so in the first place, while he was being introduced; that much was certain. Later, to denounce him as an imposter, they would have had to confess their original gullibility. And the revelation of his sex and identity might have made him one of them; cunningly hostile, perhaps they realized this and preferred to let him sit there — ignorant of their opinion, that is, half-ignorant of his own identity — an equivocal wallflower. Whenever two or three of them withdrew to the adjoining rooms, he imagined that the hilarity he heard concerned him; they giggled as if it were their common secret who he was — not his own. Rita, their hostess, who knew, spoke to him now and then but scarcely tried to draw him out of his corner.

Carl left him to his own resources. He was having a good time and was so excited that he did not look happy. Sometimes he gazed across the room with the strange smile which Philip remembered, which, perhaps, he had provoked, which now testified to pleasure that he certainly was not going to share.

The eagerness and the provoking mockery of the group of masked girls was concentrated on Carl. They too glanced repeatedly at the unhappy figure in the corner; and whoever they thought it was, their gaze expressed the hatred which immature girls feel for an older woman, less lovely, less ignorant, more sumptuously dressed. Defiantly, they grew less and less reserved. Carl profited by this rivalry with a symbol.

Having with the aid of his cousins made a girl out of his country friend, he seemed to have lost his awe of girls, perhaps even his respect for them. Rough and dreamy at once, he teased and touched them all; his impertinence seemed involuntary and was not shamefaced; apparently no one took offence. Something had aroused his marauding instincts of a half-grown man, quickened the progress of emotions about which, up to that night, he had done little more than talk. He himself had a look of astonishment at the liberties he was taking.

The other boys in consequence grew coarser in their speech and gestures, hoping, if not to outdo him, to check his triumph by embarrassing the girls. In their turn they looked boldly across the room at his supposed cousin from Milwaukee, perhaps thinking of revenge; but not one had the courage to sit down in the conspicuous corner.

Rita's mother, with great complacence, had begged them to have a good time and not to break anything, and retired to her bedroom.

The games were lively but not quite amusing. A ring on a string brought the slightly scarred and stained boys' hands into contact with smaller moist hands and even among the folds of dishevelled costumes. Humiliating positions and red-faced kisses were assigned as forfeits. A girl played the piano, but not many of them knew how to dance, and these seemed unhappy to be in each other's arms under the eyes of their friends. Then chairs were placed in a row, around which they marched; the music stopped and started without warning, and they scrambled for seats; there were pushes and pinching and needless collisions. Sometimes one or two would pause by the dining-room door to stare at the pitchers of lemonade, the plates of sandwiches and cake covered with napkins; but Rita did not want to serve the refreshments too soon, lest the party come to an end.

One of the Indians and the girl with a bunch of violets moved chairs into Philip's corner, one on each side of him. They found nothing to say. The girl's look of languid interrogation shifted from her partner to the disguised boy and back again. The Indian pulled his fingers. Then the girl rose and darted out on the porch. Glancing back at Philip with an indefinable expression, the sturdy youth followed. Through the bay-window Philip saw a single shadow made of both their figures, and supposed it was a kiss.

The party could not go on much longer in those small warm rooms. An increasing impatience for the dark and the bushes, for long grass in which footsteps would be lost, for soft boughs lost in the sky, was revealed by everyone's glances toward the doors and windows.

Carl pursued his Irish-Turkish girl from one chair or sofa to another with boisterous but somber violence. Philip waited until they reached the opposite corner of the other room, and then slipped into the hall. No one was there; the door stood open and the freshness of cut grass and blossoming syringas drifted in. He wanted to go out on the porch, but did not dare, because of the sweethearts who had just left him. He sat down a little way up the stairs, took off his gloves and his half-mask, rested his overladen woman's head in the palms of his boy's hands...

He was not alone many minutes. The boy in the uniform of no particular country followed him. Neither knew what to say; the soldier sat down on the same step. Philip knew him by sight—his father was a carpenter, his name was Art Sampson. He supposed he must have figured out his identity. Then Art Sampson took his hand and put one arm around him. Philip twisted about in confusion and changed his mind—obviously the soldier did not know who he was. He tried to get up, but one foot somehow caught in the skirt and he was afraid of tearing it. The soldier sighed with his lips pursed. Philip did not know what to do. "Give me a kiss," the other muttered. The kiss slipped off Philip's cheek into the scented strands of his wig. He got away, giving the soldier a kick, leaving him to his astonishment. The kick hurt his own foot because Lucy's slippers were so thin. He came back into the sitting room alone.

Not many of the guests were there. They had gone out by a door which opened directly on the porch. Carl was gone. Two unattractive girls on a sofa were telling secrets. Some boys were playing poker on the floor; paper flowers and streamers lay all about them, crumpled and untwisted. The remaining costumes were also torn and trodden upon. Philip stood there, miserably excited.

Out in the dark, as usual, couples mixed up with the time of night and the porches and the flowering shrubs, one girl laughing under a tree with a shrouded sound (a hard hand was over her mouth), someone trying to play a stringed instrument, secrets being told and being felt, no more misery in the kisses, no more self-consciousness in such games as were being played ... Carl was there with his Irish friend.

Everyone had forgotten Philip; he might as well not have come. He could not make up his mind where to sit down. His dress hung askew; he straightened it with boyish jerks under which the corrupted silk gave way. Their hostess, Rita, dressed as a queen, was sitting loosely on a sofa; the other Indian, a slow fellow, held her hand and seemed to be studying it. She looked feverish and disappointed.

Philip decided to go home, and wondered why he had not done so before. He did not want to say goodbye or see the boy in the hall again. So he slipped into the dining room as if to look at the refreshments, thence into the kitchen, from the back porch to the pitch-dark alley, and down the alley to the street.

There he felt frightened for a few moments. Men might be coming home from the saloons, the billiard parlor; some of them were capable of anything; they would think the worst of a woman alone at that hour, in such clothes, and tear off the clothes if he told them who he was. He walked as fast as he could. A boy's stride went badly in Lucy's shoes. He stumbled over the dress and tore it. Now he did not mind taking it back to the sisters in bad condition. He would tell them, he thought vindictively, that he had not had a good time—they would be sorry.

The wide sky, he saw, was dappled with stars. He was angry as well as tired. Carl had played a trick on him, neglected him, deserted him. He did not know whether that would bring an end to their friendship or make it more substantial, equalize it. He would make another friend if this one failed ...

Under the street lights the lawns foamed with flowering plants. From Rita's back door he had turned down a side-street to avoid passing her garden, and he did not see anybody in the others.

Perhaps if he had talked to the pseudo-soldier they would have made friends, and laughed at the fraud of the one, the error of the other. Soon he would be enough older for there to be no more disguises, nor need to be taken care of, nor harm in being neglected. He hated women's clothes; by a deliberate step he tore the ruffled skirt again.

Out of the evening's misery in retrospect faded all willingness to be unhappy. The only good time had been up in the tree at twilight, the pink satin amid the green leaves forming a world of their own, without excitement or humiliation; then being disguised as a woman had been like being a large flustered bird guarded by the branches. How long ago—it might have been sometime in his childhood. Never, he resolved, would he have such fairy-tale ideas again.

He had to cross the river on a little echoing foot-bridge to get to the part of town in which he lived. An odor similar to that of cucumbers rose from the water and the mud. There down below the brown currents were trickling, the green willows with gentle boughs caressing themselves. He no longer envied the caresses in Rita's garden. He was sick of the age he had been too long, the age of envy and masquerades, of petty martyrdoms which have a savor of joy, when nothing is satisfactory in solitude; and tried not to think that some of this youthfulness might be natural to himself and so permanent, for he wanted that night to mark plainly an end...

There was no one on Main Street. The pool room and bowling-alleys were closed. He made up his mind to go into one of these places as soon as he could save money from the small allowance which his parents gave him and get someone to teach him to play. He had looked through the windows often enough to know what they were like. The air marbled the smoke, the broad green tables under the light-bulbs shaded with green glass swinging gently, the smooth cues manipulated according to complex rules, the ivories rolling, twirling, meeting, hard cheek to cheek, with a little pure click, the men in shirt-sleeves, absent-minded, vain, and skillful;

and down below in the basement the alleys of glimmering wood, waxed and exquisitely jointed, stretching away under the great growling balls to the pins in perfect order, and the only negro in the town to set them up when they fell, his ugly face shining… Philip smiled for the first time since he had been dressed up in these rustling torn clothes. He was too young to be strong; he might never have brutal strength or direct, effective desires; he believed that he could be skillful.

He wished that he had a luxurious house like Carl's at the other end of the town to go home to—the odor of bath-towels and tobacco mounting the wide staircase with classic banisters; and the luxury he wished for was something serviceable and severe like the felt and the ivory and the waxed wood behind the shabby façades on Main Street. He wished that he had a rich mother like Carl's to satisfy once and for all his desire for such things as the satin clothing and soft foliage, in the maple tree after sunset; and robust, indifferent brothers, not to protect him but to be imitated by him. Instead it was to Mrs. Dewey's boarding-house that he was making his way as fast as he could.

He opened the door cautiously. The dirty stairs were lit by a gas-jet. The room in which Mrs. Dewey slept opened off the first landing. She called, "Who's that?" He did not answer, but mounted more quietly. By a creaking of the boards inside her door he understood that she was looking through the keyhole. She would think that one of her other boarders, the undertaker's assistant or the patent-medicine vendor, was receiving company in the night.

A Guilty Woman

IV.

A Guilty Woman

One day in midsummer Evelyn Crowe, the murderess, left the state penitentiary. It was very simple: she slipped out by a small private door with the warden, who took her to the train in his car.

She had been sentenced to nineteen years at the age of thirty-nine, and had served six. Once she had been a prominent teacher and sociologist, and the director of a settlement house in a large city. Consequently, in the prison, she had been made matron of the factory in which female convicts sewed overalls, and later a sort of secretary to the warden. In the latter position she had enjoyed great confidence and might have been privileged to run errands in the town occasionally; but for her own peace of mind, she had preferred not to keep alive her sense of the world outside the walls.

Eventually she had heard that the women's clubs had sponsored a movement for her release, making capital of the fact that her lungs were infected with tuberculosis. Petitions had already been rejected by one governor, but his successor might have a more merciful disposition or political reasons to show clemency… Evelyn Crowe had put aside these insubstantial hopes irritably, because they undid her stoicism. Nevertheless, in the warden's office, she had studied the candidates' faces: a pendulous, lucky face, another pulled this way and that, with a mouth like the seam left by an operation.

One day the warden had sent for her, and with as many divagations, as much shortness of breath and flushing as if he were asking for her hand in marriage, announced that she had been pardoned.

Free and out of doors, she was astonished by the mediocrity of her feelings. There was the immortal blue sunlight, the seedy trees in line against the brick walls, as vivid on the outside as they were leaden within, and beyond them the flimsy residences, the lawns rich with hammocks, washing, pigeons, children at play. The sight of these things did not quite penetrate her heart. For within herself as well as behind her in the prison all was still iron and cement, still hollow, everything in its logical cell, silent but for a buzz of machinery, immaculate as a hospital, organized as perfectly as heaven or hell. She did not shrink or weep, which also meant that she was strong in spite of her lungs.

On the way to the station the warden made a mournful face. He had been proud to have so remarkable a woman among his charges; she had been a perfect secretary. Nevertheless, he had lost all joy in his work while she had been there. He also was a prisoner, not by transgression, but by vocation, a prisoner of the instincts which fitted him for the high position he held. Into this spiritual confinement she had seemed to introduce tormenting sentiments of the free world—pity, scruples, fortitude. He had a habit of saying that he meant to lighten as much as possible the tragic destinies of which he was master; whenever, for example, he had thought of some new and ostensibly beneficent ruling in which lay hidden merely a desire to exercise power or even to cause distress, she had reminded him of his words. So she had robbed him of some of his vigor by robbing his duties of their perversity, and in other ways as well.

While he bought her ticket she stood in the waiting room, the only one in the state, she thought, in which handcuffed travellers were common, from which the worn-out and liberated like herself departed to begin something or another, offence or expiation, all over again. There was a large mirror under the clock. She took off the ill-fitting hat and blue veil which her friend Martha Colvin had sent in honor of the occasion. It was an unattractive old creature she saw; the small penitentiary glasses had not given back any such woeful image, for she had been handsomer and fresher than the other convicts, though by no means the youngest. Her iron-gray hair seemed to have died there, of hasty combing and bad soap and lack of sunlight; it resembled a cheap wig. The skin sagged at her temples and along the jawbones; it was knotted up, on the other hand, around her brilliant eyes, her thick mouth wasted away, her very large nose. Well, she was an old woman; in a way she was glad; nothing more could happen to her; life would be comparatively easy.

The train whistled. She and the warden went out on the platform. It stopped at the junction and whistled again. The warden hurried back to the waiting room and looked inside. "Will you kindly step this way a minute, Miss Crowe?" It was second nature to obey his peremptory voice. Inside the door he pulled her about by the shoulders and kissed her. She might have laughed or cried or both if the train had not been there to hurry her away.

She found an empty seat in the car and wrapped the blue veil about her face, expecting to be recognized. Once her picture had been in all the papers day after day for weeks. She remembered having happened to see, on her way to prison, the gaunt and blotted face crowned with headlines rolled over and over and torn by the wind in an alley. Just having looked at herself in the glass, she realized that those blurred half-tones were better likenesses now than when they had been made. But of course no one even wondered who she was, who six years before she had been.

So life would be comparatively easy, but thanks less to the short memory of men than to Martha Colvin. They had gone to school together, and Mrs. Colvin had been a widow for fifteen years; she lived alone outside Brussels, Wisconsin, and made a good living by farming. Upon the news of the crime she had hurried to Belleville to keep her friend company during the trial, and upon the news of the pardon had invited her to her house.

One could not get to Brussels by railroad except through Belleville. She changed trains at Milwaukee, and as she drew near the scene of the disaster station by station, her heart grew heavier and looser until it felt, inside her shirtwaist, like a sponge. She put back her veil so that she could see clearly.

Hills looking down at the train, in groups reclining against each other; cattle in flocks lifting their noses out of the grass to look; groves in which they had gathered chestnuts, as a pretext; roads raced over by a certain phantom automobile—oh, now the driver was dead… The brakeman came and went, crying "Belleville" through the car.

It was there that as an untroubled spinster she had come to teach history in the high school while she wrote her book, *The Unmarried Woman Worker.* She searched for the house she had lived in, unsuccessfully; had she forgotten which one it was? She moved to a seat on the station side of the train. Red clapboards, a scale for weighing wagons, cinders on the planks, taxis pale with dust drawn up, small factories and grain elevators, the click of the telegraph, and a slight moist noise somewhere of welcoming or parting kisses. "All aboard…" The train crept away.

She had hoped to see a familiar face, however painfully familiar—not a one. A Civil War veteran with a series of little dishevelled beards and withdrawn, weeping eyes, looking, looking, not seeming to see much. She would like to have had a glimpse of one of her pupils, a boy named Philip who had sent her magazines and several books while she had been in prison. Getting sick at his stomach in his father's harvest field when the newspaper with her name in large letters had arrived—so she had thought of him ever since; it had been midsummer, a day as hot as this. At that time he had been the chum of the nephew of the man she had killed. Captain Fisher—unworthy, unlucky man. Bill…

A woman sat down beside her and remodelled her mouth with a stick of rouge. Someone had given her rings, which had settled well into her plump fingers. The sort of woman he had preferred, she thought, perhaps one of the very ones. Her lawyer had offered in her defence proof of his immorality, most of it new to her; and had complained afterward of her cynical expression during this part of the testimony, which, he said, prejudiced the jury against her. Now she regarded humbly and even with admiration this woman, fleshy and at ease, who had known how to keep young, and wished she could begin a conversation.

To the left the courthouse steeple rose like a weapon toward the cool, round clouds. There she had been tried. Extra editions of the newspapers had been sold on the lawn for those who had not been able to get into the courtroom. The steps had been crowded with reporters and women, women with mouths made firm by appeased love, successful jealousy, with fortunate bodies filled out by child-bearing.

The train got up speed; a hill had covered the steeple. Now both crime and punishment were behind her; little that meant. The young woman at her side licked the rouge off her lips and fell asleep. It took three hours more to get to Brussels.

There was Martha Colvin waiting beside a little automobile. She held Evelyn by the shoulders and studied her appearance. "You are not old," she said.

Evelyn knew that she was never going to be able to express her gratitude toward this impassive creature with strong, freckled hands, red-mouthed and sallow, in an untrimmed felt hat and a baggy suit.

They passed between fields of straw which made of the dusk something yellow and animated like candle-light. Indifferent to them, but struggling against wave after wave of other emotion and of weariness, Evelyn described leaving the penitentiary: the formalities and the goodbyes; and how the warden's man of all work, a simple-minded negro serving time for rape, left alone with her in the office for a moment, had sung several bars of a spiritual, his loose joints keeping time—"Oh some o' these mornin's bright and fair-air-air, I'm g'wan to lay down this weary load"—running out into the long corridors when the warden returned; and how she had seen no one whom she knew on her way through Belleville; and even how the warden had kissed her in the waiting room. Upon hearing the last anecdote Martha's face darkened, as if her friend's troubles were beginning all over again. Evelyn did not know how to explain that she could not be susceptible to love anew, that she was safe. They decided upon a pseudonym and a false identity, lest the hired girl spread the news of her arrival about the neighborhood.

Martha's was a wooden house with piazzas and a lean-to summer kitchen, a grape-arbor and a stone creamery, under a pair of elms like two big shrouded harps. In the yard there were fine poultry and a sleeping cat, and hollyhocks with dry leaves and cheap-looking flowers, red and rose. Martha took her up to the spare bedroom and said, "Make yourself at home."

Any private dwelling would have seemed like a wooden snail-shell. Evelyn was afraid of the great Wisconsin thunder-storms, no longer shut outside quadruple walls, and for a long time could not sleep because of the sounds that there are in nights of liberty.

Martha said: "Now don't you worry about a thing. What I've got is yours as long as you need it. I hope something will turn up after a while, because we might get on each other's nerves — we should be a sorry couple of mean old widows, sitting here trying to outlive each other."

"I can never repay you. Anyway, who am I to think of such a thing? There was a time when I devoted my life to others — or thought I did. Now I'll just have to say thank you, and do nothing else in return." She was kept from weeping by the fact that it would have embarrassed Martha.

"Well, that doesn't matter in the least. But you ought to do something some day; for yourself alone, not in return. Something that will take a lot of energy and be of great interest. Your life is not over; it's not enough — to do wrong and be punished and get out and then to sit around and think back."

"You'd be surprised to know how little I think."

"So much the better."

Evelyn had never known anyone in Brussels and was still too timid to meet strangers. In fact, she did not want to do anything. It seemed enough — to make friends with the country, the storms, the domestic animals. She had forgotten them, and they did not reflect upon her exceptional evil life as human beings would have done. The rain falling upon the just and the unjust alike … She had indoor habits; needless to say there had not been a comfortable chair in the prison.

She went to see a doctor in Milwaukee, who told her that her lungs had begun to heal in the prison and would give her no more trouble if she led a quiet life; tuberculosis had been only an internal scar of the bullet which, between five and ten minutes after her crime, she had directed against herself, which had torn away half of one breast and a fingertip.

The days were long in idleness. Every week or two Martha, accompanied by a man named Bolton who was her dearest friend, went hunting or fishing, according to season. The house was full of firearms. One morning Martha said: "Wouldn't you like to come with us? It seems to me you used to be a good shot. Didn't some doctor once tell you to do it for your nerves?" Then she realized her blunder, turned scarlet, left the room, came back immediately. "Dear, my dear. What nonsense I talk! Please excuse me."

"Thank you for forgetting," Evelyn said.

The two women lived alone, without guests, for several months. At last John Bolton came to supper. He was an old bachelor doctor who owned some property in the town and had virtually given up his practice. Before Evelyn had come there to live, he had been in the habit of spending the evening with Martha at least every time they went hunting together. Therefore, uncertain whether or not she herself welcomed the distraction, she was happy about it for Martha's sake.

Martha introduced them. There followed an extremely nervous silence, from which Evelyn gathered that he knew who and what she was. They sat down to supper. Martha tried to talk about their last hunting, about the crops; the doctor seemed unable to pay attention. Evelyn determined that they were not going to spend the whole evening in this way. So she said: "I have been hungry for six years. Penitentiary cooks, as you may imagine, are not the best in the world. Everything tastes so good…"

The doctor felt obliged to smile, cheerlessly.

With desperate patience Evelyn told what they had had to eat, and then continued about the prisoners and the prison, speaking as if she loved them above all other people, other places. With desperate patience, in which panic rose between every two sentences, hard to put down… If she had to stop, she thought, she would have to leave the room. The doctor resembled some one, the warden perhaps—perhaps because they were the only two men she had talked to in years. Suddenly she began to recover some of the joy of her lectures, her classes, her life as it ought to have been; two pupils, one of them hostile, the other tongue-tied with anxiety and compassion…

Little by little the man's face relented; it grew less handsome and more like Martha's. He stopped holding himself away from the back of his chair. He began to eat heartily. He asked questions. Martha's eyes reddened; she smiled at them both as if it were she who had reason to be grateful. From the prison they turned to other subjects. There were two or three minutes at a time when Evelyn forgot that she had ever been a prisoner. The clock struck twelve before he thought of going home.

The next day Martha went to town, and Evelyn was restless. She had read and reread all the books in the house; she could not learn to enjoy sewing. She remembered Martha's having said that she would find a pile of old magazines in a certain clothes-closet. There they were, over Martha's half-dozen mannish dresses; large popular monthlies with rose-petal girls on the covers… Hall Caine, Phillips, new names—she smiled in anticipation, thinking how bad literature justifies itself by treating more important matters than good writers have the courage to touch upon: violent sentiments, adultery, ostracism, guilt, and redemption. She carried the dusty piles to a rug in the middle of the floor, sat down among them, began to turn over the pages.

One magazine was fat with a package of clippings, and opened of its own accord; the package fell out. It was the newspaper record of her crime and trial. What she felt was her idle smile hardening into a mere twist of flesh against her teeth. Shabby, yellow, carefully dated pages… All during the trial she had wanted to be able to observe how it was going, how much of the inner truth was made clear — but as in a dream her mind had seemed to be floating, slow, cold, extraneous, and to understand any given moment she would have had to stop it in its flight, to give her attention time to thaw out. Now she was going to know everything, whether she wanted to or not.

There were the photographs of herself which had become good likenesses long afterward, in weird hats of that time. Photographs of her father, now dead, whom Martha had persuaded not to visit her in the jail. The settlement house, so discredited by her connection with it that soon after it had had to close its doors. The house in which she had lived in Belleville — it looked like a pile of match-boxes with a turret. The staircase and the hall with a large X printed on the carpet. Captain Fisher, Bill…

That carpet had been red with intertwined violet flowers. There he had lain, in a shirt changing color, a coat getting wet; large, blond, abominable. And loved. Less loved then than at any other time; it was her love that she had killed, too violently, too late, and he had died only by accident, died because, having good luck with love, he had bad luck with everything else — he had always said so.

Having told him a new reason for them to get married, having listened for she did not know how long to laughing abuse, she scarcely knew what — she had bounded up the stairs to a certain bureau drawer, driven by something beside anger, and darted down again, agile, senseless, her entire outstretched arm one weapon, stiff and tipped by the pistol. Then she had not looked at him but had telephoned the superintendent of schools to come at once. There had been two more bullets in the pistol—not enough. Shooting herself had been a means of getting the body out of her sight, the body abominable for two reasons: because it was good-looking, brutal, and frivolous (his fault), because it did not rise out of the dark pool in front of the door (her fault). The superintendent of schools had found her sitting on the stairs with the pistol pointed at him, a spot on her shirtwaist, waiting, then growing tired of waiting, ordering him to look the other way, firing again, hurting her hand, missing again, fainting.

All this, she saw, had been in the newspapers; testimonial proof of it, comment, and illustrations. Her heart was like a churn; she was breathing out loud. It was not her guilt which she minded, guilt without premeditation; but for a doctor's advice she would never have possessed a pistol or any other weapon; a day's delirium, unpardonable—but after all, she had not been pardoned, not for six years. Unfortunately there was something more in the papers.

There were her love-letters. They had been printed serially, word for word. They were genuine; she remembered having written them; she had never seen them. Where had she been when they had been read in court? She heard, as clearly as if someone were standing beside her, over her, a famous man saying in an active dry voice like a grass-hopper's, years before that, "You have remarkable literary talent, Miss Crowe, Miss Crowe, Miss…" She believed that if she had ever seen those letters she would have choked herself to death in the jail with her own hands, half a finger missing from the left hand. "Does he long for his teeny-weeny"; love-nest and sick craving and bed-time; "Oh, how I miss you…" She had called him daddy, sugar, big bear; she had spelled out baby-talk; crosses for kisses.

She began to cry, but it was only a sort of rustling in what was left of her breasts, something like a fist clenched and pressing upon her tongue. She had forgiven the man; this was merely being unable to forgive herself what they had had in common, she told herself—but it did not help. What they had had in common was vulgarity. After years of waiting, in haste to be corrupted, how womanly; purity preserved until the day after her thirty-eighth birthday; a woman of a certain age; the age of reason; when love brings drunkenness...

The crime had taken ten minutes; these letters stood for more than a year.

"I just thought I'd try old maid's love—see what *that* was like," he had said, just before the end. What it was like... Misspelled, indecent, idiotic. "Old maid's love, old maid's love," she cried aloud. She pressed her face against the pages of the magazines, tore at the rug with her nails. Everyone she would ever know had read those letters.

Having come thus far in her thought, she made another discovery. Her mind seemed to open; it was like pages opening of their own accord; love fell into sight. If she went on seeing John Bolton...

In her imagination shaken by sobs, dusky with tears, the doctor's face took on all the moving aspects of other faces, the dead man's beauty, the warden's authority; it even borrowed kindness from Martha's. Face flowering in her exhaustion... Suddenly the wild dream put her to sleep, and she lay, with her head on the magazines—in which, like any other reader but more than any other, she had found the history of her life, past and future—until it was dark, until Martha, sounding her horn in the lane, came home.

Evelyn sprang to her feet, put back the clippings and the magazines, threw herself on the bed to leave a hollow in it, and went downstairs to tell Martha that she had been taking a nap. If Martha learned what she had seen, what had happened, she would not forgive herself for having kept the clippings lying loosely about. Never, she must never, never by a slip of the tongue... Perhaps that was the only thing she would ever have a chance to do out of gratitude.

For two or three weeks keeping the secret was not easy. Thus far she had been saved from shameful, even from regretful, introspection by the hardness of prison life and by the fact that, since nineteen years was a life-sentence, nothing mattered, and lately by the shock of freedom. Now, a free woman but falling in love, she had to look at all her conduct clearly; love was a cruel brilliant light within herself, upon herself, focused as if by a magnifying glass, burning, fiber by fiber. A personal, portable hell…

She pretended to be merely ill. Martha studied her, suspicious of vague sicknesses, and advised her to consult Dr. Bolton. All day long her rough-looking lips were restless with questions. Evelyn, yearning for a confidant, was afraid of them; at the first deft inquiry all the anguish might come out, with the least word she would be doing harm again—she had done enough. She discovered that by not trying to deny to herself her desire to talk to Martha, and putting it off from hour to hour, she could accomplish her end, and by hiding her newly awakened shame, little by little lost sight of it herself.

But she determined not to see the doctor again. The next time he came she stayed in her room. Martha said: "John thinks you don't like him. I don't see how you can help it—he is nearly perfect. Anyway, I didn't notice that you didn't, the other night."

"Oh, but I do, very much. Quite the contrary, I thought he didn't like me. A woman who has shot somebody must be prepared for that."

"Stop saying such things, I tell you," Martha answered, sharply. "I don't know what has possessed you the last few weeks."

So Evelyn persuaded herself that it was Martha who persuaded her to see the doctor. Old and hopeless though she was, the autumn after the first frost, the Indian summer, was like a rustic heaven—the part of heaven in which not all desires have been fulfilled—the forests blushing and rusting, all the hours full of hesitation, of waiting, of hope. John Bolton came often, and at last often when Martha was not there.

He said: "I like you because you can change. You grew old, and now the last few weeks you have been growing younger. You have been a foolish woman and at other times you are wise. I suppose you had strong feelings but sometimes I wonder if you aren't cold all the way through—you think all the time. Then sometimes I notice the fiery way you speak. Perhaps that is because you were a teacher. Or perhaps because you were shut up there so long with only your ideas to see—you do talk of your ideas as if they were people. Now Martha and I have been the same every day for about thirty years."

She said: "I changed too much, one day, in a few minutes. Coming from the prison, as I passed through Belleville—that was where I—that was where it, happened—I looked up and down the station platform, to see if there was anyone I remembered. There was nobody but an old soldier with whiskers. He was looking up and down the platform. His eyes were rather murky. I think I am like him in a way—he must have lost the past by losing his memory, at least the memory of what made him do what he did and he was looking for a future to take its place, to fill the vacancy. No one spoke to him."

"Oh no," he said, "they took you away to prison just at the age when women get old. Your hair is grayer than mine or Martha's, but you seem to me the youngest."

She said: "I am as good for nothing as if I were old. Martha wants me to get back my ambitions, my ideals. Indeed, I don't want to be dependent on her always. But the fact is I feel as if I should never want to lift a hand again as long as I live. You see, modern prisons are arranged for people who commit crime for profit, and out of laziness and cowardice. If hard labor gets to be a habit for them, maybe they will have the patience to earn a living honestly when they get out. This system made me lazy and a coward. For I feel that I did my share under lock and key, I mean of hard work—and I don't know what else but physical labor I should be allowed to do now. Don't forget that in the old days I was paid a salary for my character, my high moral standing. You can imagine how little there is left of that."

"More than you think. There is some kind of superiority about everything you say, everything you do, your eyes looking straight

at people, the way you lift your hands without touching anything.
You are different."

She said: "I may seem to be, but I haven't been. I know. Because,
not long ago, I saw some letters I wrote. As you see, I lose my voice
when I try to speak of them. Sometimes I think I mind because
they make me like everybody else, because I was proud of the
exceptional aspects of my life, because pride is my besetting sin.
Sometimes now I decide it would have been better if I had been,
from the beginning, more like those letters, like other people, a
little vulgar all the time instead of holding it back. Waiting, oh,
complacently, for the dam to burst. Disastrous old maid…"

"Don't—" he said. "You know, you haven't been living in
Wisconsin in late years, not right out in it. Or else you'd have more
pride, by contrast. You can't imagine how stagnant we all get. We
use the most miserable language and so we can't understand each
other. But we are all alike just the same. We are all so countrified
and disappointed, although everything succeeds. You must have
travelled a lot when you were young. When we get to my age and
have plenty of money, we'd go away, but we don't know where
to go…"

One night they were playing pinochle. Martha had gone to bed.
The house cat sat purring on Evelyn's lap; in their hands the cards
whispered; they were tired of talking. The out of doors, brought
close to them by an uncurtained window, was bluish and cold.
She shuffled and dealt. Suddenly John dropped his cards and took
her wrists in his hands; her cards fell in disorder; how tired they
were of playing!

The table was covered with a piece of buckskin, an entire hide
with a bullet-hole under her elbow. The cards were pretty under
the warm lamp. The ace of spades, Carmen's death—her sad old
eyes hunted for it and failed to find it; without meaning to, he
had covered it up. *A dark man will come into your life. I see a
long voyage…* These were the rulers over this world, the powers:
different denominations of power, spotted red and black, shuffled
and thrown down under clasped hands; the calm red-yellow busts,

bedizened, not smiling, each one with two faces, always right side up, always wrong side up—it did not matter which. She could not think of anything but what she saw, and resolved to have, all her life, a pack of cards spread out where she could see them.

He held her hands for a long time in silence. Then he said, "Evelyn, wouldn't you like to marry me?"

Martha's cat sprang to the floor as she stood up. For no reason they hurried over to the window. He said: "We are both lonely. I can take better care of you than Martha can. I am fifty, you are almost as old. We'll go away. You'll be happier."

"Don't tell me reasons," she interrupted.

"Please. Please, Evelyn."

"Oh, oh, did you think I wouldn't?" she cried. "What am I—"

They had come across the room to the window, that is, to the one-sided, scarred wintry moon. It gazed at her for a long time like some soiled omnipotent face, now weakened by her weeping, now flashing with her emotion, now hidden by John's face…

"Will you leave me now?" she asked finally. "I can't understand, with you near, how all is changed."

"You tell Martha," he said. She loved him the more for not being courageous at that moment. He went home, yielding her to her joy.

Her own courage was scarcely sufficient the next afternoon, though she was not aware of all they were doing to their friend. John was not coming until night. She and Martha sat together, well bundled up, in a patch of late-November sunshine, under the stripped arbor. "Martha, I love John. He has asked me to marry him."

Martha wept. She wrung her gloved hands and covered her face with them both.

All the one's hope being flooded away in the flood of the other's tears, all her joy crumpling up… "Then," Evelyn muttered, "you yourself, you too—"

"Don't mind me. It's all right. It's wonderful. You won't stay here, will you? It will be all right."

Evelyn spoke sternly. "First, tell me if you love him. You *have* loved him, all the time."

"Oh, of course I loved him. Who could help it? Fifteen years…"

Evelyn said: "Then I won't. I can't. It's very simple. I will go away. You shouldn't have let it happen. If I weren't too old I'd take my miserable life now. Please, please forgive me now, Martha. And help me to get away soon."

"Nothing of the sort. You're going to marry John. That's that. And say no more about it. And you're going to live happily ever after."

"How odious! Wicked I've been, never as wicked as that. You came to my rescue twice. Oh, my shame!… Compare me with yourself. The murderess turned thief—"

"Stop! Evelyn, stop at once!"

They sat for a moment gazing at each other like strangers.

"Now I must explain," Martha began again, "why I've been kind, since that worries you. The misery of other people makes me miserable. I do what I can to stop it—for my own sake. That's all. I've had good luck, within limits. Because I've been prudent. Well, I hate prudence. But if I manage to do something for others, you, for instance—why, I don't have to be ashamed of myself. Pride is my besetting sin. That you must understand, that I am a thoroughly selfish woman."

Evelyn was thinking: two kinds of selfishness, Martha's and her own; Martha's was not likely to be rewarded on this earth. As for herself, she did harm unintentionally—but thoroughly—and when it was over, aroused sympathy and secured help. Which meant that her disastrous emotions were not so foolish as they seemed. She made use of them, as of a kind of unconscious cunning, to get her own way. She was the more feminine of the two; therefore hers was the winning side, the winning side. Nothing succeeds like success—odious. "No, no, no, no! This one thing I can't, won't do…"

Martha paid no attention to her. "Now about John. You know, at first he wouldn't come to see you. On account of—oh, well, you can imagine. I made him come. In order not to have to respect him less. Then it occurred to me that this might happen; I thought of what you told me about the warden. That's why I left you alone together—you see I always have my reasons—in order not to have to reproach myself for the jealousy I did feel. I hoped you were both too old to think of marrying, and then we'd stay here together, all three of us. Now of course you will travel. I always thought you should go abroad where even you couldn't expect anyone to remember the past. I thought of lending you money to go but, I couldn't afford to; the crops have been poor for several years and pork isn't worth anything any more—"

"I can't sit here and listen to you talk like this," Evelyn cried. "You are proving how much better you are than I am. Oh, better, better, I should think so—and you can't keep from making me feel it. You might have spared me that. I am ashamed enough. I can't endure it. Stop it for the love of God!"

"Evelyn," her friend said quietly, "we are too old to quarrel about a man."

Evelyn held her breath. This was the realm of violence—she recognized it, she had been there before. The territory of murder. And having come to it again, there was nothing there to drive her mad. There was nothing there at all, except pity and timidity; a wistful look on the woman-farmer's freckled face, as if she were asking a favor, a little of a certain kind of irony or mockery to hide the look. Life had no curse left…

Patiently, Martha began again. "I can't remember when I didn't love him, and in all that time he never once asked me to marry him. He asked for—and received—other things. Oh yes, he is fond of me, I know, I know. But there was nothing to keep us apart; there was also nothing to bring us closer together, nothing to provoke him. It was always quite all right as it was. For him, I mean. And since I always supposed this might happen some day, I realize that when you told me I behaved disgracefully."

Not by the words but by the tone in which they were spoken, the emotion with which they were heard, Evelyn knew that she could not be frustrated or defeated, could not defeat herself, even if she wanted to—could not want to. In the old days she had not known her rivals, unless that was one whom she had seen in the train, years after, coming away from the prison. This then was the rivalry of women, this, invincible love. Blessed are the hopeless and the guilty, for they...

Suddenly, to her amazement, she found herself rejoicing at the superiority of her life over her friend's: her friend's life in which there was every personal virtue, every lone self-sufficient virtue, somehow cut off, somehow condemned to renunciation; her own life grasping and surreptitious, without kindness, without wisdom, but wedded to an old destiny, putty in its lover's-hands, vapor in its arms. Old, old as they all were. Her thought ran on to her own ends: John—an indulged and optimistic man—could she make him as happy being what she was—but never more an old maid.

"I bore him to death," Martha said. "I know it. I have always bored him. You don't. That is your reward for what happened to you, for having been—all that. He will live to be an old man now and be young to the end. He wouldn't have but for you; I know him, and shall bless you every day of my life. And I don't need him. I assure you I don't need him. You do. I've always been too proud to need anybody—it serves me right."

Evelyn tried to protest once more, half-heartedly. "I deserve nothing. I am a spoiled woman. Let me give him up, make me, let me be good at last."

"Listen to me. It doesn't matter whether you deserve it or not. The rain falls on the just and the unjust alike. And if I took him away from you I shouldn't be keeping him, for I've never had him—and what would you do? I don't want to be responsible, I don't want to interfere with what is one of the advantages of your destiny, I refuse to. We can't all of us do what we like."

Indeed, there was no choice at this parting of the ways. The unfortunate one of the two could not choose more misfortune, nor the fortunate one happiness. Evelyn could not expiate the evil she had done; Martha could not profit by her noble lifetime.

It was late and growing colder. The two aging women kissed one another. The scenery of their hearts was exactly like that of nature in the dusk—a violet hollow well-swept of clouds, the ashes of the year making the air strong, trodden autumnal paths leading infinitely apart and away. Their cheeks were very cold because they had been wet.

It was time to go indoors and make haste in the kitchen; whatever the circumstances, men had to be fed. John kept them waiting, and when at last they heard him in the lane, so much did Evelyn admire her friend that she was afraid and held her breath. He might have regretted the choice he had made between them; he might be coming to tell them that he had changed his mind.

The Dove Came Down

V.

The Dove Came Down

It was a Sabbath morning in the prosperous town. It was mid-winter. At the end of each ray of sunlight melted a lump of snow. Down the glassy walks men and women in black and brown wool, leather, and fur, tripped stiffly between the banks of snow which, in the center, had a radiance of blue glass.

Arm in arm Arthur Hale and Emily Grover went to church together. They were engaged to be married, and she was there visiting his large family for the first time. He had no particular faith, but she was attached to the one in which she had been brought up; and they were taking refuge in that church from the constant attention and inconsequential embarrassment which resulted from her presence at home.

They found a vacant pew at the back under the south window where the strong sunshine, falling upon their backs, would keep them in mind of the perfect weather outdoors, as purely bright and troubling as the relation which brought them there together. But the memorial windows somewhat spoiled the sunshine with their rainbows of raw color. The false rafters and the pews were newly varnished, the plaster newly painted and stenciled. There was a mixed fragrance of rubber galoshes, wet woollens, and houseplants which bordered the rostrum.

The pastor looked happy and progressive, but when he took his place in his armchair, followed on a sort of balcony above and

81

behind him by the organist and the choir, he assumed a dolorous attitude with one hand over his brow. Then he came forward to the pulpit, ran his eyes over the satisfactory congregation, and lifted his very gentle voice in prayer.

"Now let us rise and sing hymn two hundred and thirty-six." Because Arthur had to lower his voice lest it attract too much attention among the breathy, inexact, longing voices, he noticed the dejection or weakness or mere poverty of temperament of the people around him. They were in large part mothers with children, old men and women, more often than not alone, spinsters in twos and threes; he looked in vain for a man of his age.

During the emphatic, sensible sermon he kept his eyes fixed on the girl he loved. She was a foundling, adopted by a virtuous man and his wife in a remote part of the state; and her large eyes had kept the humble and shining look, her lips the resolute sensibility, her voice the eagerness to please which those of orphans have. As a lawyer in the second year of practice he earned only a modest living, but as soon as some one could be found to take the country school she taught, they were going to be married. Her profile there at his left, tinged by the stained-glass sunshine, no higher than his shoulder... The little nose was almost transparent at the tip. Upon the wilfulness of that little chin, as if upon a cornerstone, he could safely found a home full of children, and a tranquil life. The mauve-and-rose mouth, listlessly attentive...

Haunted not by the past but the future, so tired of having waited six months already, they were almost unhappy together. This merely showed, the thoughtful lover believed, how mighty and singular happiness would be when at last, at last, he should get enough of looking at her, and shut his eyes in her presence, when they should no longer have to make conversation, but instead their mouths should fall asleep, half open, tasting fragrance, full of warmth...

The alto and the soprano of the choir rose to sing an anthem. Girl-priests—perhaps he ought to have known them, but black caps and gowns took away their identity. They were tall and sober. One of them had an olive complexion with a bloom of rouge; the

other's face was a face for the theatre, which would be lovelier
the farther away you were, as long as it could be seen at all. Their
voices, immature and sophisticated at once, touched the young man
and made him blush; so he took Emily's black-gloved hand in his.
The entire congregation rustled in the pews. An old man parted
his lips a little and struck his teeth together, very softly. Everyone
seemed ready to make a sacrifice of something.

During the anthem Arthur suddenly noticed that a table was
spread below the pulpit. It was the morning of Holy Communion;
if he had known that he might not have come. Some one's best
linen falling to the floor; the Body and the Blood, plates of bread
and trays of drink under fresh napkins...

If only he and Emily were out on the country roads which were
probably lively with shaken sleigh-bells and shaggy horses steaming
at the mouth—they could put their hands in heavy fur mittens on
each other's knees.

Four middle-aged men awkwardly went down the aisle. The
pastor removed the linen, blessed the spiritual nourishment, and
sent them back to the congregation with it. A dead silence fell in the
high, bare room. All the women took clean handkerchiefs out of
their bodices and handbags. Silent prayers were offered—doubtless
for the healing of sicknesses, the straightening of deformities, the
breaking of bad habits, the return of wanderers.

The young man began to suffer secretly. Unwilling pity,
unreasonable awe. Oh, that every prayer might be answered,
every yearning appeased, so that one might be at peace with one's
sweetheart—at peace with the yearning for one's sweetheart, if
nothing more! But he was ashamed of this amorous selfishness.

The summer before he graduated from law school, taking his
vacation in France with several friends, he had gone to Lourdes.
A great sunny square in front of an ugly church. On two sides of
it, at the back, in the shade, the families, their eyes full of tears;
in front of them a regiment of wheelchairs, and in front of the
chairs, in the blazing sun, in beds on wheels, grotesque bodies that
seemed to have been made of candle-drippings, a little bit alive,

arms and legs wonderfully tied in sailors' knots, luminous heads like overturned pieces of sculpture with broken pedestals swathed in bedclothes. Hundreds of them, of all sorts. Mass was being sung in droning tones all around the square by powerful, unshaven priests. Others held their arms out straight from the shoulder in the attitude of being crucified or flying. Others went from sufferer to sufferer, pouring the holy water into tin cups from receptacles which looked like kerosene-oil cans.

(In the Wisconsin church the shoes of one of the men who were handing round the sacrament creaked on the fiber rug. All their shoes carried moist tracks away from little puddles of melted snow.)

For the people in Lourdes there was only one thing to wish for—death. But the church had neglected to teach them how to wish to die. Everywhere rose instead a hopeless demand, rose like a gas, like a loud cry, like a soul more than life-size, let loose; a demand for a miracle of healing to come down, on wings, there in the middle of the square where the ground seemed to be heaving; so fierce a demand that the air palpitated with it and rang in one's ears—or perhaps that was an effect of the heat. Arthur had felt sick and gone off by himself under the great plane-trees, behind the crowd, to wait until his friends should have had enough.

That was a Catholic mystery; this was merely symbolical worship in a progressive Protestant church. That was visible need, mutilation, desperation; here it was invisible—not quite invisible, the difference was not great enough. Miracles were all alike—but had there been a miracle, would there be one? The minister had preached about the Holy Ghost's coming down at Pentecost; interpreted it lightly, hopefully, in terms of brotherly love, public spirit, and pacifism. The startled apostles around a table, the Dove with ruffled plumage in midair, in a nest of little flames—so it was in the pictures. Not caring how the pastor had explained it all, Arthur thought he understood what it meant.

Directly in front of him sat an old man; the nape of his neck sparkled a little with close-cropped hair. A vigorous old man, worn away to the bone by hard living; and he was shedding tears like a young girl, with the same gentle steadfastness.

Nothing could be done to prevent it, Arthur thought—his life must be going the way of the lives of all those around him. The way of the impermanence of joy and the reiteration of pain. So that the day would come inevitably when he too would be crippled in one sense or another, and lose little babies, and suffer odious disappointments; innumerable days of illness to be healed, deformity to be strengthened, bad habits to be broken, wanderers to be longed for; the day when Emily would die. Would he come here, then, following his neighbors, to the Lord's Table? Where divine grace did or did not come down...

Meanwhile the silver platters of rectangular crumbs, the trays of little purple tumblers, went up one row of pews and down another, doing their work, such as it was.

The dove that ought to come down... (The organist kept playing a series of roving, lamentable chords.) A bright beak, a swelling, palpitating throat, glowing wings, snowy and silky, wrinkled red feet with glassy claws—tearing the husk of disappointment off such satisfactions as there were, tearing the present away and leaving the future bare in one's arms (in the spring he and Emily could get married) breaking, in order to heal, the miserable body (his body left behind when Emily died). He turned his head so that his eyes could run up to the top of one of the windows where several panes stood open, hoping to see a pigeon, a sparrow, anything with wings—for good luck.

He remembered a thing that had happened when he was a small boy. He was lying on the lawn with his eyes almost closed, peeping at the clouds—he had asked his mother if the clouds were angels; she had laughed—and a rooster following a hen, not seeing him in the grass, ran over him. It leaped and gave a guttural squawk, flapped its wings, and scratched him with its feet. He had cried all that afternoon; he remembered and almost felt his terror.

The church was hot. He wished that he had not come away from his father's house. The nerves in his body seemed to be striving to pull apart; it was misery to sit still. Emily's face was entirely lacking in expression; he supposed that if she lifted her rather bluish eyelids she would smile at him, seeing nothing of his trouble. Somewhere behind him a steam-radiator hissed softly like a sacred snake.

Vaguely he remembered having read something in college about the origin of this sacrament. Magic and the beginnings of religion... A priest by the fire, among the curls of his uncut beard moving his weathered lips, rolling his eyes. (In his armchair on the rostrum the pastor seemed to be saying a prayer for himself.) Chosen bulls and the finest of the flock led up. The handmade knife on the very soft throat. Thick jets of blood. Recitations by the priest. Smoke almost too heavy with fat to rise—that was food for the god. Brutal men falling upon the hot meat. Charred but still wet bones being quarrelled over. Angry panting, sighs of happy appetite. Uninvited guests at the meal of the god. The best cuts for the bravest. With the god's blessing. That was not what he was trying to remember.

The ugly stained-glass windows, discoloring Emily's cheeks, irritated him unreasonably. They ought to be broken, and the pieces sent away into the jungle for the missionaries to give to savage tribes.

There in Africa and the islands, other rites, fundamentally the same. All around in the dark beyond the camp fires the thick wreath of forest with, here and there, lionesses and leopards, by way of flowers in the wreath. Sleeping sickness, marauding beasts, undernourishment, leprosy—they need all the divine help they can get. The most aged of the men plays priest, a vigorous old man, by a hard life worn down to the gesticulating bones. (The nape of the neck of the old man in the pew ahead was strangely checkered by deep creases.) Drums in despair: the dead hide beaten, the bodies beaten, the earth beaten. Dance of old women, the older they are the keener the frenzy, the higher they leap. The feathers and dead leaves they wear limp with sweat, gray with kicked-up dust. And there is a feast at last. Eating the enemy, in order to usurp his magic and absorb his power. Eating the god. Eating the body of god—that was it, that was what, in his overexcited mind, among his college memories, Arthur was hunting for. What the sacrament meant...

He tried to think of the man, the Jew, the beloved of the whole world, who had instituted the particular feast at which he sat— "my Body and my Blood"—one man who was a god and did not need anything for himself, not even a miracle; but, for more than a moment, he could not.

The sacrament was going down the row of seats in front of him. The old man took his share, smiling through his extraordinary tears. His own turn would come soon. He could not take it. What would Emily think? She removed the black kid glove from her right hand. There it was. Emily put the morsel of crustless bread between her lips and took one of the fragrant cups; Arthur hated her having to. Then, feeling for one moment like a renegade, a foreigner, an impotent, he passed on the plate and the tray.

Emily looked up at him; she gave him a little smile, wistful and—oh, he could not be wrong, he knew every one of her smiles—proud. She was proud of him for having refused.

So the rest of the service passed quickly, in the reaction from his excitement and the joy of her smile. There was another hymn; there was a benediction. They were going out with all the congregation. Emily knew no one; he bowed now and then, but coldly, in order not to have to speak.

The noon sunshine, snowy and silky, fluttered and wheeled about like a flock of doves larger than any on earth, covering the whole town. Every bit of glass or polished metal in the automobiles and the windows hurt one's eyes and then made them feel refreshed. All the snow-banks were shrinking; the water froze again on the walks between them, so that they were like straight streams of glass on the edges of which trees threw down their shadows, dim chains and wiry crowns. Arthur asked, as they went down the street, "You didn't mind, did you, Emily, my not taking communion?"

Her lips already forming the word No, she merely smiled, hoping to hear his explanation.

"It's not just that I'm not religious. An ancient, terrible, important thing that is. Blasphemous to do it, without being willing to; I should almost have been afraid. Even if I were religious I don't think I should want such forms of worship. They seem like asking for what one hasn't any right to ask for, at least as long as one can get along without it."

"Ritual, I mean all the emotional parts of religion," Emily said, "are either a comfort or they hurt a great deal. Oh, religion can make one so unhappy when one is young!"

"But it doesn't make you unhappy ..."

"Oh no. But it used to, long before I met you."

They were walking down the long, bright, shabby main street of the town. Little heaps of popcorn in a booth between two shops gave off an odor of harvest, butter, and heat, an odor which meant hunger not keen enough to be painful. Arthur wondered what his mother had prepared for them at home.

"Did I ever tell you how I got religion at a revival meeting?" Emily asked. "I must have been about thirteen; I know I had just begun to grow tall and was often a little sick. My foster-father is very devout, a sort of mystic. He was especially strict with me on account of my origin—he seemed to think my real parents had not been very religious, nor even moral, perhaps."

She smiled up at her lover's frowning face. "Well, one day a revivalist came to our town—I've forgotten his name, but one of the famous ones. He brought his own quartet and hired the Opera House for three nights; all the Protestant churches combined to finance it. My foster-mother thought I was too young, but my foster-father insisted on my going. The Opera House was the hall where they had moving pictures and dances and two or three singers and entertainers every winter. I had never been inside it, though when I had to go to the dentist I used to peek through the keyhole. At first I was disappointed; it was a big sad place like two or three empty barns thrown together, and had a strange smell. But I soon forgot where I was; I had never been so excited in church.

"He called himself the Soul-getter. He had a rich pleading voice, but sometimes it grew harsh, filling the hall, thundering, making quite grown people feel as little babies must when they are scolded. His sermon was very long and very wonderful, everyone thought so; about how badly people were behaving in recent years, about moving pictures, about drinking, immodest dresses, and dancing, and what these things led to. I didn't understand it all, but listened eagerly; I did not dare look at my foster-mother, for I felt sure that she would disapprove of my hearing such things discussed. Not a great deal about hell fire, but some; and at the end he talked of Christ's crucifixion for us, and how horrible it was not to take advantage of it.

"Then he sat down to rest, and the quartet took his place. I had never heard such beautiful singing, mournful and complicated, and it made me have a lump in my throat.

"As soon as they finished he leaped to his feet again and called for the grace of God to enter people's hearts and implored every sinner, every disbeliever, every sufferer, to come down to the front and be saved. Not from hell—he didn't say anything about that during this part of the service—but from sorrow, remorse, loneliness, disease, shame, and such things. How we would do wrong without meaning to; how those we loved would die, and no one but the Lord to comfort us; how having no faith was like an awful sickness; how life was all suffering; how we are pitiful and ignorant. He would talk like this for a while; then suddenly he would shout, 'You must be saved! You must be saved! Come to the feet of the Lord! The blood of the Lamb, shed for you! Come down to the front! Come all ye!'—repeating everything over and over. He waved his fists and rocked back and forth as if he were beating time to what he said. First at the top of his voice and then in a whisper; sometimes it seemed as if he were going to break down."

"I think..." Arthur began; but Emily would not be interrupted.

"At first I was frightened and wanted to run out, but of course I couldn't. My foster-father was sitting between me and my foster-mother. I was only thirteen and young for that age. I dreaded growing up, anyway, because my foster-parents were old and I would be alone in the world, which I thought would be like another Orphans' Home, even larger and even more badly run. I began to think of my real parents and how they had left me at that orphanage, where the punishments were so severe; and I had never seen them and perhaps they weren't living. Please understand, Arthur; no religious feelings, not one, but the most frightful emotion. I hadn't felt anything like it since the days in the Home when I used to get so tired, doing what the matrons made us do, that I would throw myself on the floor, whimpering and kicking. Meanwhile a great many people did go down, some crying, some repeating the speaker's phrases. He came down off the platform and met them, and helped them kneel down, not ceasing to speak. It went on and on."

Arthur looked as solemn as if she had made him angry. "I think," he said, "I believe—that the most important virtue, the thing we need most and ought to learn how to develop—is stoicism."

"But that is not the end of my story," Emily said. "Suddenly I burst into tears; I could not help it. My foster-father turned toward me and whispered, 'It is the grace of God.' I cried all the harder. Then he spoke out loud. 'The grace has come into your heart. Suffer the little ones to come unto Me. Don't cry. Come up to the front. My little daughter, come with me.' What could I do, how could I tell what was the matter? People were turning around to look at me. He led me up the aisle and made me kneel with the rest. He held my hand. I could not stop crying. The revivalist pitied me and patted my head."

They had walked from one end of the main street to the other. It looked very gay, though nothing had been meant to be beautiful. Behind the plate glass of the closed department stores brightly dressed manikins struck attitudes, up to their knees in great leaves of frost. Other windows were softly white with steam, and one might have said that these were weeping. The drug stores had put out their racks of magazines which resembled old-fashioned flower-stands, with the faces of film stars for flowers. The sky let fall its blue and white on the banks of snow and the painted buildings and the sweethearts who now walked in silence, very soberly, though there was the gaiety of wreaths left from Christmas for their eyes, the cheerfulness of several shouted greetings for their ears.

Upon Emily's face shone without question a faint smile, the faint certitude of love; but she seemed to have grown tired as she had told her story. Her shoulders had straightened as if she had taken upon them something heavy. Now Arthur felt the dependent pressure of her arm in his, and saw that her feet were unsteady; only the feet of a strong young woman going toward her lover's home—but they were like the feet of a soul moving, with a certain fortitude but dubiously, amid religious mysteries, fears, and abrupt visions, a great distance from any other footsteps since in that realm, however much love may do, no two human beings can agree.

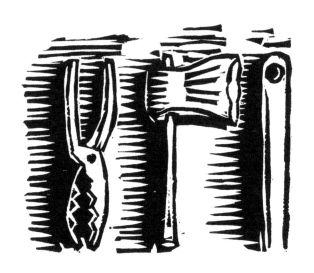

Like a Lover

VI

Like a Lover

Stealthily, on Summer nights, a young girl would creep out of the house (her mother asleep behind one door, her uncle behind another) sitting down on the carpeted stairs and sliding from step to step, remembering every loose board and graduating the pressure of her feet upon them, leaping from the threshold into the grass, shrinking behind a tree—her eyes fixed on the bedroom windows where a match might flare, on the doors where one of them might appear—then darting across the lawn and running, running until a man came out of the hazel bushes to take her in his arms.

On those hot nights the sleepers lay without covers, muttering and grinding their teeth. Mosquitoes pressed against the screens. The pans of milk had been placed where the draught between two windows would keep them from turning sour. The cattle grazed on the hills as if it were day. Moles and rabbits shrank against the sod, and owls hooted, rolling their yellow eyes and snapping their beaks which were like pairs of curved scissors.

In the lane between ripening orchards the lovers, a slim girl and a man of middle age, spoke little, and when they did, the broken phrases mingled in the shadows with the chirping of crickets; and as they embraced, the girl often shed tears.

Her mother had forbidden her to speak to this man. Alice Murray was too young to be thinking of men, and he was nineteen years older than she. Alice had admitted that she liked him, and her mother had said that she would die of shame if anyone found it out. Because, because—no one knew why.

He was a widower named Hurst who had come from Iowa and rented a farm near Hope's Corner, Wisconsin. He had not been trusted in five years. He worked hard, he was saving, he did not drink; his housekeepers were always old women to whom he paid no attention. But everyone wished that he would move to another part of the country: not because he never went to church (others were without faith) nor because he was not sociable (others were sullen). Someone said that he could not keep a dog; all his dogs ran away and took refuge in other people's barns.

Then Mrs. Murray had found out that Alice had been walking with him in the evening, and had told the girl that the next time she disobeyed she would be put out of the house to shift for herself. Alice had listened, sitting very still with her hands in her lap, and had seemed to be looking at something the mother could not see. Mrs. Murray had said that her soul was sick, and she would come to a bad end. Alice had listened as if to an announcement that someone was going to die—a pet, a friend, a relative, herself maybe—but of course everyone had to die, so what could one do? Finally her mother had wept. She was a hard woman; her husband had been dead a long time; the brother who worked her farm was a weak old bachelor whom she had to govern; she was like a man and wept like one, her head bent over between her knees. Alice had wondered how she could explain that she was helpless; but she could not explain, could not promise, and could not weep. She would have liked to. Paralyzed... How could she make her mother understand that? Her mother had said that if it ever happened again she would have to whip her terribly. The girl had hoped that her mother would not find out what she was certain to do; that had been all she could have said, and she had not dared say that.

The summer had come, and continued. Leaves swelled that would be wilted by the frost; corn ripened that would be ripped from the husk; the lambs and young cattle fattened that were to be butchered. These things happened inevitably.

And in the same way the flickering of a certain charm in his eyes was inevitable. They were round eyes with rays of clear yellow shooting out from the pupils and red veins radiating over the white eyeballs—she saw them when he struck a match for his pipe. If he kissed her cheeks, they held, as if in a little pointed scar, the memory of his mouth. If he stretched out his hand, she responded to the touch before it reached her. If he had told her to sing, there under the ragged elms, she would have straightened and sung, whoever heard, like a whip-poor-will. When that bird sang—each throb of sound seemingly the equivalent of a throb of pain—she imagined herself singing like it, making music as bold, as wounded, at his bidding. But he told her only to be still and not to think.

Then he came back with her to the garden gate where the elder blossoms hung like delicate handkerchiefs, and embraced her there; and she, who had crept out of the house with so many trembling precautions, returned as confidently as if she were walking in her sleep.

She had oiled the hinges of the door of her room, and not being latched it swung back noiselessly at the pressure of her fingers; and she tiptoed over the threshold, the pupils of her eyes dilated for the darkness. But there was no darkness: a lamp rolled low—her mother—her mother—getting up unsteadily—something in her hand. She remembered her mother's warning, and by the glow of the lamp (the flame on the wick making a little noise, *pruh, pruh*) she saw and in one second understood the face like a wooden mask, the unbalanced steps, the uplifted arm … She saw without seeing clearly, dazzled by the delicate light; and her mother had not yet crossed the room, but she was very near.

The girl gasped, fell on her knees, and threw her arms around the other's knees. Her mother whipped her with the strap. A voice in the girl's mind kept saying, It does not matter, it does not matter—but the strap cut through her thin shirt-waist. When the strokes of the arm over her head were regular, she could catch between her teeth the cries which rose; but when a stroke, disturbed by the mother's weeping and incoherent words, fell out of its turn, and when she remembered that only a minute had passed since she had left her lover (and she saw him standing between the garden gate and the clump of elderberry blossoms, like handkerchiefs) she began to scream.

Her uncle, unable to endure it, slammed his door and stumbled down the stairs and went out to the barn.

At last the mother also sank to her knees, and they embraced, sobbing, as two women after an accident (two women strangers to each other) weep, clinging together.

But all the next day the girl waited with perceptible impatience for the night; so that her mother was desperately aware of the minutes hurrying one after another, and whenever the clock struck, she shuddered. They were sitting in the grape arbor by the road when a man came down the hill on foot. Alice knew Hurst at once; her arms stiffened along the arms of the chair. Past the cherry orchard, past the stable, past the garden … Then her mother recognized him and stood up abruptly; the mending in her lap fell to the ground; and she bent over Alice as if to protect her or detain her, putting one hand on the girl's shoulder, and turning her face so that she could see the man if he approached them, but need not look if he were passing by.

Would he stop? Now Alice was sure that he had heard her cries the night before; and what had he come to say? Both women held their breath … He was passing by without looking at Alice, he was giving all his attention to her mother, he did not seem to see that she was there. The mother's eyes were like two bits of glass, the man stared at the mother, the girl at the man. And then Alice observed on his face a curious expression, whose meaning she could not begin to understand: an expression most like that of envy.

He was gone. Tears ran down Alice's cheeks. Her mother said firmly that the following day she would have to go away to visit an aunt who lived in Waukesha.

During the afternoon Alice took a screwdriver from the tool-box of a mower and put it under the mattress of her bed, and hid some matches and a candle-butt in a pitcher. After supper, as she had expected, her mother led her up to her room and locked the door. Alice waited until the house grew still, lit the candle, stuffed paper in the keyhole, laid a skirt along the crack under the door, and with the screw-driver unfastened the cheap lock. Then she blew out the candle, and crept down the stairs as she had done night after night, but trembling as never before, trembling like a phantom whose hour has come and who is about to disappear.

By the time she found Hurst in the orchard lane she was weeping, shuddering, and stumbling; but gradually she grew quiet in his arms, because they held her like a great rope and there was no room for violent emotion. He kept repeating quietly that now she must stay with him and marry him and never go back to that house. Then he comforted her, calling her "poor baby," and she cried again, partly because of the pain and partly because the words reminded her of her childhood, now at an end; but nevertheless she could not think of returning to her mother after what had happened.

The next morning they took the train to Waukegan, Illinois, and were married. She was happy for five days. On the sixth she received this letter from her mother:

Dear Allie: I don't think I can stand it to see you. My heart has been bad again. I guess you'll have a hard life. If you need me I'm still your mother.
– Your heartbroken Mother.

After that she was often afraid. She stayed at home always, for Hurst seemed to prefer it; furthermore, she did not want to meet her mother and uncle though she often cried with homesickness, and she never crossed the road to the barn without glancing up and down to be sure that no one was approaching. Their nearest neighbor, the only one who came to the house, was a school friend older than Alice who had married a farmer named Clifford. This woman stopped whenever she drove to the village, and asked enigmatic questions, staring into Alice's eyes with anxious avidity, as if afraid that something was being kept from her: something phenomenal, something dangerous, the commencement of something inevitable...

Alice was often afraid, and she began to notice the whips and heavy clubs standing about in the corners of stalls and behind the cattle-stanchions and on the back porch. Her husband took pride in his tool-shop—the saws, adze, pliers, and chisels, polished and in faultless order—but she disliked going into it; if she needed kindling, she looked for sticks that she could break across her knee, and when she had to drive a nail, she did it with the heel of a boot or a stone. The house was comfortable, though obviously the only women who had lived in it had been hired help; but there were no flowers or pets, the cattle were not named, and her husband had no pictures of his relatives to show her. She never went into the barns without calling his name first, and tried not to wonder why. When night fell her vague terrors came to a climax; but she always went to sleep beside her husband, thinking that she had married too young, thinking that it was mature life which brought with it constant fear and a little pain—never blaming him.

The charm disappeared from his eyes as she went on living with him, and he seemed smaller and more like other men. No longer was she under a spell—they were man and wife, and he took her for granted; but since she had married him, the circumstance of marriage itself held her in a kind of paralysis.

But she lived with him only about five weeks. Though she did not expect to be happy in her marriage, she had not thought of going home—perhaps never would have thought of it—but for what took place on Sunday, the fifth of October, in the night. The next morning, after Hurst had gone to the fields, she wrote on a piece of paper which she left on the kitchen table:

> I cannot stay here any more. I have gone home. I believe you know why.
> If you don't know, you can come and see me. Your wife.

She went on foot, trying not to arouse the curiosity of those she met, and running when the road was empty. Her strength lasted until she saw her mother standing on the porch at home, but she fell to the ground then, with her hands over her eyes.

One year passed. No one knew what had happened. No one talked of anything else. No one could decide whether or not Mrs. Murray knew. Hurst did not come to see her. Scarcely anyone spoke to him except on business; he became an outcast without leaving the country, and seemed not to care, though he never raised his eyes to look anyone in the face.

Another year passed. Once more Alice did not leave her home, and looked up and down before she crossed the road, avoiding her neighbors and dreading the sight of her husband. She began to be called Allie Murray again, instead of Mrs. Hurst.

Three years... From her porch she could see the road that came down from his farm and always recognized his horses. During that year she saw him within speaking distance upon four occasions; they did not even bow, but she was ill each time for several succeeding days.

Four years... Hurst divorced her. She never spoke of her marriage, and indeed spoke very little about anything. She took in sewing, but could never learn to do more than the simplest things, such as undergarments, gingham dresses, and children's clothes; and when she had nothing to do, she sat on the porch.

Five years... She looked like a woman who has never been married. New people sometimes did not hear of her marriage until they had been in the community two or three months. She was stronger than her mother now, but seemed as old. She looked like almost any woman and might have been of any age.

Six years... She lived like a woman who has never been married. She had a canary and two cats which gave her great pleasure. Mary Clifford came to visit her every week or two, but when she gave up trying to find out why Alice had left her husband, they had little to say to each other. Her uncle died, and they found a steady hired man after having tried two others. Her mother kept the entire responsibility of the housework, because Alice was absent-minded.

Seven years had passed. The evergreen, which before her marriage had been a small thing, like a feather set on end, was now a tree with tufts of needles moving and sighing on every bough. Seven years which had seemed very much alike, though some people said that the winters were milder now and the springs began earlier ...

Then a young widow named Mrs. Clayburn came into the community as a seamstress. Alice heard of her first as a rival, for women who would not have thought of going to a new and more expensive seamstress for work that Alice could do, spoke with interest of the newcomer to annoy her; but she did not care. Mrs. Clayburn lived in Bellville, a town about six miles away; Alice lost no customers, and forgot her very existence until one day Mary Clifford said it was common knowledge that the widow was going to marry Hurst. As she said it, Mary Clifford seemed to grow very small, like a doll, a little thing which danced up and down; and a voice, Alice's own voice, cried out to her friend, so infinitely far away, "What does that mean to me?" and suddenly Mary Clifford was saying goodbye.

That night she lay awake, reviewing the events of those five weeks, seven years before, mechanically, as if it were a story she had memorized, and before the dawn lay in the east like a bouquet of flowers on a threshold, decided what she ought to do.

"I am going to town today," she told her mother. After the noonday meal, she put on her best dress of brown cashmere sprigged with violets, and brushed her long hair (strands of iron-gray, strands still bright, like rust on the iron) and pinned it up in a figure-eight, and stood for a long time before the mirror gazing at her face, twisted almost imperceptibly here and there by flaws in the glass. How different from the face of her girlhood—for she was thinking of the past: the pupils of her eyes very heavy on the lower lids, the mouth as firm, as much like a man's mouth as her mother's. Her mother had had such a hard life. Had she (Alice Murray, Alice Hurst) had a hard life? Almost no life at all—five weeks. Five weeks, and now ... For her face was different also from that of the day before: a faint blush in the hollow of the cheeks, and in the eyes which had not sparkled for years, a motionless luster. She tried to part her lips in a smile, as if determined to begin to be once more what she had been so long ago; but she was too excited even to imitate a smile.

As she drove away from the house, the plumes on her hat, like the tails of two miniature squirrels, trembled more than the motion of the buggy alone would have made them tremble. She was resuming her life, and felt the pride of all women with a warning message. No longer was she merely a married woman who was like an old maid; no longer was she one of those neglected personages whose mystery has been forgotten as all insoluble mysteries are, one of those friendless creatures who have experienced but one thing—the thing of which they dare not speak.

Her face which had resembled the face of almost anyone, now wore a remarkable brightness—experience which was hers alone suddenly seeming to have been concentrated there, glowing on her strained lips and feverish cheeks, shining through the dullness of her eyes in which tears had been too often restrained, weeping freely at last. Now and then a man stooping over a bundle of grain in a field, paused, wondering "what Miss Allie was up to"; or a woman on a porch would call to another indoors; and for a moment, here and there along the road, her enigmatic life would be remembered—but not as she remembered it. Her memory, thus aroused by circumstances, was like a hallucination; it startled her again and again. She clutched her hat; her tears dried suddenly in her eyes; and she did not see the glittering straw in the harvest fields, or her neighbors who spoke to her, or the children of those who were so fortunate as to have children, playing by the road.

She drove into Bellville. This was the house; a family she had known in her girlhood had lived in it. The soft maples, the plants in the garden tied with strips of cloth, the stoop-shouldered porch—she saw them less clearly than she remembered them. But her friends, not friends any more, were not there; a stranger had taken their place, a stranger to whom she was bound by an intimacy more extreme than ever united friends. As she knotted the tie-rope about the horse's neck, her hands shook with the embarrassment of a recluse forced to become an intruder. But she crossed the lawn to the door with assurance, as if her errand had made her young, at least as young as she was.

She knocked. Just inside the door stood a little child—she had not known there was a child. Its hair was yellow like straw, and, stretching out its hands, it made the gesture of the Child on the Virgin's knees which Alice had seen in pictures in the parlors of German Catholic families. It kept repeating in a faint sweet voice syllables she could not understand. Her tears started again, and she pressed her fingers against her lower lip, thinking she would have to run away over the lawn, and down the road, and home.

But her knock had been heard. Mrs. Clayburn came into the hall and stood beside her child, which hid its face in the mother's dress. She was a pale, strong woman wearing a red dress; blond hair in numerous puffs encircled her stolid face; she gazed at Alice, mildly. "Please come in," she said.

Remembering that she would be expected only to order a dress, Alice crossed the threshold. The young widow indicated a chair in the parlor, took the child in her arms, and carried it to another room where the sound of a sewing-machine ceased, and returned. "I am Mrs. Hurst," Alice said.

In less than an hour, seeming to brush away a veil before her face, she hurried out of that house. And she drove down the road, urging the lazy mare, "git-up, git-up," slapping the reins against the dashboard, shielding her eyes against the light and against the hard fence-posts passing in two processions. It was so hot, the summer would soon be over. She had been so defeated, she could not suffer indefinitely longer. She thought, It is autumn, the men are taking in the harvest; and thought, I know what the end will be, and it will not be long coming.

"I am Mrs. Hurst," she had said; and then, not knowing how to go on, she had asked, "What is your little girl's name?"

"She is called Lily," the widow had answered. "Why have you come?"

There had been a clock ticking, and the strokes had seemed to be irregular. "Why have you come?"—once more.

Then Alice had asked if it were true that she meant to marry Hurst.

"What is that to you? You aren't his wife any more."

Alice had begged for an answer, her eyes resting on the hem of the other woman's skirt, for she had thought of throwing herself on her knees.

"You want to be his wife again. Jealous…"

Alice had protested, and had explained that it was she who had left him, that she had been divorced because she had left him, that she had never spoken to him since; and had insisted on telling the other what had happened.

Mrs. Clayburn had straightened in her chair. "You needn't. I'm going to marry him no matter what you say."

Alice shivering, protesting, threatening vaguely… The other woman standing up, standing in the center of the room, her face extremely white, wringing her hands. "Leave my house. Coming to spoil my life. I won't have it. This is my home. Go away!" She had stamped her feet. "Go!" She had pleaded: "Mrs.—Mrs.—Hurst, please go!"

Driving down the road, Alice remembered every word, her own words: "I won't. Not until you know."

The widow had sunk drearily in a chair, her mouth quivering, her dry, opaque eyes fixed on Alice; and she had breathed, "What happened then?"

"I was afraid. I loved him. Loved him as a child loves its father. I mean I was in his power. Helpless, very young. My mother whipped me when I ran away. I was only eighteen." Alice had whispered as if she had been ashamed.

Mrs. Clayburn had tossed her head impatiently so that one curl had shaken loose, and fallen open like an opening hand. "Quick. What happened…"

As Alice had continued, the other, the one whom she had been there to save, had crouched in the chair and had smiled. "Fool," she had murmured. "Fool. He wanted to scare you."

Alice had wept, and the sewing-machine in the other room had sounded again like an enormous bee. She remembered afterward how her own voice had sounded, the words almost inaudibly rattling one on the other, lifting, dropping, like hundreds of leaves broken off at the stem. Leaves blown over his feet as he had gone off to work seven years before...

"Go on," the other had whispered.

And at last the woman who had whispered had panted as if with the fatigue of an intolerable confession, and Alice had wept quietly as if she had been the listener. The young widow's eyes, shining and liquid with fear now, had not left Alice's face for the fraction of a second. "But he did not know what he was doing," she had said. "Walking in his sleep..."

Alice had answered quietly, "He knew. Before I went home to my mother the next morning I wrote a letter, saying that I thought he knew why I couldn't stay with him, and if he didn't know he should come to see me. He knew. He never came."

Then, for the first and only time, the young widow had screamed—a brief sound muffled in the palm of her hand; and Alice had known that she knew, that she understood, and that she believed. Shaking her head mechanically, the widow had gone on murmuring, "But I've got to do as I must. But I've got to do..."

Alice had implored, threatened, and pleaded. Her loud words, certainly loud enough to have reached the next room where the sound of the sewing-machine had ceased, had been interrupted by a little whisper: "Can't help it. I can't help it. I wish I could."

Then Alice had leaped to her feet and had stood over the other woman. The other woman had cringed, pressing her cheek against one shoulder. Alice had lifted her hand to strike her.

And in that moment the other had said, "I am powerless. Paralyzed..."

Alice had stopped, her hand in the air. *Paralyzed*… A stupor like a cold veil had risen in front of her eyes. Then, in the heart of the heat of an afternoon she had seemed to be sitting, her fingers loose upon her knees, listening to her mother's threats. And how pitifully she had tried to yield on that occasion, as one who is dying tries to let another breath enter the scornful nostrils and rejecting lungs, but she had had no will-power; paralyzed… In her mother's parlor (in the young widow's parlor) there had surged over Alice Murray (Alice Hurst) a lethargy, a lassitude. Was it herself, the inert creature in a red dress on the cushions? Was the one who stood with her hand uplifted over the other's head her mother, or was it she? Who was it who was weeping with anger? Which was she?

She would never forget the body of the other woman outstretched in the great chair as if flung down by violent hands, with no expression in the face but a disdain for expression, and a disdain for movement, and a disdain for all that meant to disturb her where she lay, peaceful, stupefied by the peace of an invisible embrace.

Alice had stared at her own arm, raised to the level of her chin; it had fallen to her side; and she had hurried out of the house.

She thought, slowly and vaguely, as she drove home: One day, out of certain eyes (eyes with flecks of yellow radiating round the pupil) one day in the center of certain eyes there burned a will-o'-the-wisp, and there was extended a promise not of joy or peace or any allurement, but a promise of what was ordained, what had to be. And what could one do?

She heard, in the beat of horse-shoes and the rattle of wheels on the gravel, voices protesting—her own voice identified with her mother's, saying, "You must not, you dare not!" And as she listened, the uproar in her mind died down; there was a hush, an end of crying and protesting; she held her breath, waiting, and knew perfectly well: What has to happen will happen surely…

Then in the yellowness over the stubble a song-sparrow lifted its voice, invisibly and in vain.

She remembered a preacher, a little man with a child's smooth, ardent face, saying that one of the five points of faith is predestination: a decree from eternity respecting all events, God having ordained in his omnipotence the happiness or misery of every one (his face had grown pale as he spoke) the passion, the marriage and death, the agony of every one. God like a lover, waiting, stepping out of the hazel-bushes in the dark, opening his arms...

You did your best. You did what you could (mothers and widows and girls). And having failed, you drove down the road alone, slapping the reins on the hindquarters of an old horse in an agitation like that of a dream; and the harvest fields swam by, and the sparrows sang in chorus, and the heaviness of the sun, loose there among the majestic trees, was gradually brought to earth... She had done her best. Nevertheless, Mrs. Clayburn would marry Hurst, and she would be killed; it was sure to happen, it had already happened—in secret, in Alice's mind.

The road led down to the river, and on the bridge her hands tightened involuntarily on the reins, and the horse stopped. Down from the north between the ghostly willows the water came in a foul, sluggish flood, going down to sunken places, each one lower than the one before, not to be withheld from annihilation in the last sunken place. As it went it rippled softly up and down its infinite length with a sigh of satisfaction. Alice watched a branch which came down, turning and staggering slightly on the surface, one branch marking the motion of the whole stream, large and full of débris. There on the bridge, her eyes bewildered by the palpitation and the weaving of the water, she wept—the last weeping there was to be.

As she drove into the yard, she wondered if she would have the strength to look into her mother's querulous face, to change her clothes, and sit down to supper, and clear the table, and dry the dishes... But all these duties were accomplished at a great distance from her mind, and suddenly she found herself sitting on the porch alone. The great, gilt sunset stood on the hills, reflecting nothing. Over its painted glitter many bats, like little black hands without wrists, fluttered; and among them a hoot-owl mourned, hunting above the meadows, around the barn, and down the lanes.

All over the darkness that night there were passive images: the most violent movements stopped in the moment of their climax; hands and incredulous faces, male and female; floating debris on the perpetual flood. Hallucination melted into nightmare. She seemed to fall asleep with her eyes wide open, and woke staring at the dawn which lay in a little, reddish heap on the horizon.

She waited on the porch. Sometimes Mary Clifford visited her, driving down the road which passed Hurst's house with a lame, white mare which nodded its head and tossed its gray forelock; and while she was there, Alice scarcely felt her fear in the effort she made to conceal it. At last the day came when Mary Clifford said that Hurst and Mrs. Clayburn had been married. Unable to be surprised, unable to feel sharply anything in which there was no surprise, Alice was content. It was as if she were listening to a long, too long story; she knew what the end was, but it went on and on; and there could be no peace until the last words were pronounced.

Two months passed, which seemed as long as the seven years. She stared up the road which led along the edge of the Hurst farm to Mary Clifford's house. The end would come from that direction, down that road; Mary Clifford would bring the news. And as she watched, dark spots would form in the empty light, and on the spots insignia would shine; a pair of scissors, a pitchfork, or an axe, most frequently a knife. She grew familiar with these things, and with all the ghosts which visited her: the motionless woman in the armchair, the eyes with flecks of yellow on the iris, the child which kept looking out of a door, making the gesture of the Christ-Child in a picture; and she grew tired of them, so tired at last that she longed for the day when, leaving her nothing to wait for but the end of her own life, they would come together and then vanish.

The last day ... Alice looked up the road. Her sight was failing, but she saw a white horse coming down the hill. Over the hedges and through the trees she saw its shaken mane and forelock, as if someone were waving to her with a large gray handkerchief. It moved with unusual speed; and then she saw Mary Clifford almost standing in the buggy—leaning over the dashboard—whipping the lame, white mare. Alice, fainting away, fell backward on the porch.

In a Thicket

VII.

In a Thicket

The mist thinned and broke like a cobweb in the May sunshine. A young girl opened her eyes; through the window beside her bed they rested on a cloud of plum-trees in flower. The little house in which she lived with her grandfather stood in a thicket of trees, blackberries, and vines. She saw the vapors of the past night gathered in the form of dew upon some cabbages and lettuce in the garden, the black crooked trunks sustaining the weight of blossoms.

She was troubled by a memory of the night, a memory in fragments. She had been aroused suddenly by sounds which her mind, confused with sleep, could not identify. The moon, submerged in mist, had swept the cottage with a whirling and opaque atmosphere. She had lain still, her heart beating fast and loud.

Then, another movement—some footsteps on the porch. Seemingly padded, they had been separated from one another by silence. Was it an animal? Too heavy for a cat, too elastic for a dog... Were there wilder beasts in the thicket? The door between her bedroom and the door opening on the porch stood open. Her speculations died down with her breath. Something pressed upon the wire screen of the window. It brushed against the screen door and seemed to shake it by the latch. It paced back and forth, a soft persistent prowl.

She had trembled with curiosity and fear. An instinct warned her that it was not an ordinary thief. She would have liked to rise, to see, to know; her limbs would not respond. The night, both gray and dense, unnerved her. Subdued noises and movements persisted irregularly for what must have been an hour. Once she heard them sweep across the grass to the back door, also hooked from within, and return. But her vigilance had relaxed; waves of unconsciousness blotted out whole sounds and moments of hush... Suddenly she was awake in the tranquil sunshine.

In the kitchen her grandfather was moving about in a pleasant odor of eggs and butter. For several years the orphan, now fifteen, had lived alone with the old man—a schoolmaster who had saved, out of the miserable salaries of his lifetime, enough to provide for their needs. She found him on the porch, last autumn's wild cucumber vines flecking his face with shadows, his hands in his lap.

"Good morning, Lily," he said, in his sweet high voice.

"Good morning, gran'pa." She kissed his cheek where it was cool and like paper above the white beard, and crouched on the steps at his feet.

What little they had to do was as simple and solitary as a movement brought about by the sunshine which dropped delicately upon the fresh leaves, vegetables, the strawberry bed, grass, birds, and petals. They were shut off from the road, from noise and passers-by, from the sight of other houses, by the grove which opened on one side only, on a wheatfield bounded by trees.

For two years Lily had not gone to the district school because of the age and remote dwelling of her grandfather, who taught her, easily and informally, at home, where she turned the pages of his library broodingly and with vague disappointment: books of history, letters, and particularly of natural history, such as the notebooks of Audubon and Agassiz. Meanwhile he wandered in the grove or on the lawn, or farther afield. His hands always clasped behind his back, he went humming and whistling about. In the early twilight they worked together in the garden, upon the products of which, with those of the hencoop and with wild nuts and berries in season, they lived. His existence had shrunk into the circles of trees, and he was content with their noncommittal beauty, their concentration. But the girl's eyes sometimes ran darkly along the horizon.

"Are you ready for breakfast, child?" the old man asked. When they had eaten, he polished his silver spectacles on a corner of the blue tablecloth, arose, and took down a Bible from a small shelf of its own. Slowly and firmly he read a chapter of Revelation.

If there had ever been an interruption of this morning worship, Lily would have dreaded its return. Today her emotion revealed itself more clearly, as if a carving in low relief had moved outward and detached itself from the stone. The tumult of coarse feeling and unknown crime which agitated the old text disturbed, even offended her. She remembered the night and the intruder. Her grandfather knelt by his chair, she by hers.

"O dear heavenly Father," he prayed, "mould us to do Thy will. Let our feet ever walk by the light Thou hast given us. Do not let them stray into temptation, or be stained by sin. Dear Father, we come to Thee humbly, knowing we have been evil—covetous, quick to anger, lusting for power, licentious. Do not punish us according to our deeds, but forgive us according to the sacrifice of Thy dearly beloved Son."

The girl's thoughts wandered, excited by the solemn beauty of his voice, by the obscurity of the words. What was it which had wakened her? What did it want? Where was it now? Should she ever see it, ever know?

"And bring us at last into Thy heavenly house, to abide with Thee forever. Amen."

As Lily washed the few dishes and placed them on the lace-papered shelves, she heard voices on the piazza, and found her grandfather talking to Mrs. Biggs, a woman who sometimes came to do their cleaning.

"And what had the man done?" he said.

With a cunning look at the girl, the woman ignored his question. Having come out of her way to bring him the news, she felt obliged by the presence of this eager sober child to omit many details. She sighed disappointedly and squinted at the sun, red hands upon her hips, and merely outlined the story.

A negro had escaped from the state penitentiary. On the edge of a town not far away, it brooded over this flat countryside: a lofty, hideous fortress of brick with a row of poor trees planted against the red walls. From tower to tower, night and day, guards walked upon these walls, which were separated from the building by a bare courtyard in which every shadow was immediately visible. At night one of the towers upheld like a lighthouse a gigantic lamp which twinkled into many bedroom windows, a reminder of all that was mysterious and shut up, over the forests, marshes, farms, and melancholy black dense hemp-fields.

Lily blanched and withdrew cautiously through the door.

The negro, imprisoned some years ago for a crime of violence, had seemed, in the prison, so subdued, so contented, that he had promptly become a privileged trusty. He drove the warden's car, and sometimes went about the town alone upon errands. From time to time he was visited by an obscure excitement which, indicated by a greater degree of gentle sadness and by low fitful singing of spirituals, was taken to be religious or even penitential. It had been thought best to restrict his movements during these emotional fits; but the day before, in spite of a very nervous condition, the warden had carelessly sent him to the post-office. He had left the car less than a mile from the prison, and disappeared.

Almost immediately the surprised authorities swarmed over the country, expecting to take him by nightfall. But they were disappointed; the felon was still at large. He had been wandering around all night. He was loose now.

Lily listened in a storm of excitement. It made nothing more clear; the relation of the news to her experience seemed insubstantial and incomplete; but she felt that the obscurities which had troubled her—the unknown, the difficult, the hypnotic—were likely to be revealed at any moment, in a flash of light emanating from Mrs. Biggs. She shrank into a chair.

But Mrs. Biggs only repeated each fact several times, panting with eagerness. She lowered her voice and rolled her eyes. And at last she reached the end of her information, her variations, and paused.

The silent moments prolonged themselves in a twitter of birds and fowls. The old man sighed and stroked his beard. "Well, poor man," he said, "I suppose they'll catch him."

Mrs. Biggs asked loudly, "Aren't you at all afraid?" For the second time the girl saw a surreptitious glance moving in her direction.

"Oh no," he returned mildly. "We are simple people, poor people. We have no money. We haven't anything he'd want."

Then with some degree of respect but a suggestion of mockery, the woman asked, "Do you like to live here in the thicket, so far back from the road? I've always wondered why you did it."

"Well, I don't know," was his absent reply. "I'm used to it. I've been here a long time. We don't get any noise and dust from automobiles, and the birds come here."

Slowly he descended the veranda steps. Mrs. Biggs hurried off with her burden of alarm; her shawl caught upon weeds and bushes. In the sunlight his beard glimmered beneath the honey locusts. Lily went about the silent house trying to devote herself to the interrupted everyday tasks.

At dinner her grandfather was silent and aloof. He had his days of a preoccupation which the girl called "growing old." It arose within him, pure, unannounced, and unearthly; it was like the radiance which a candle-flame shoots through the wax beneath. She wondered if the negro's sad spells were like his. She knew that he had forgotten the morning's news, that he brooded upon nothing known to her.

As the afternoon passed by, a globe of light and fragrance, his mood deepened and darkened. For a year she had endeavored to understand it, with only vague and indirect conclusions. Was it sadness at the expenditure of his life? Loneliness for those whose knowledge was simultaneous with his? Was it memory which troubled that mind like a pool, as if sunken things arose and floated on the surface?

His eyes seemed to turn away from the trees, clouds, birds, shadows, garden, away from her—to look within. He worked only a few minutes, but paced around the garden and sat in a wicker chair, shading his eyes with one hand.

Under the trees beside him the girl mended some clothes. Her courage sank low and lower, but persisted. The sun declined in the plum-trees. Acute rays came between the trunks of the thicket; those of the poplar became silver, the birch pink, the ironwood black. In silence the voices of some geese, trembling through the air, set up there a vibration like themselves.

She arose and kissed her grandfather; his face was smooth, cold, and frail under her lips. "A good girl," he murmured. Should she tell him about the night? For she was sure the negro would return. What was to keep him from coming in? Nothing, nothing at all.

As she thought of the situation she found resources in herself which she did not name. Her ignorance provided no concrete images to nourish fear; furthermore, something within her implored the indefinite to break open, to take shape. In her courage there was curiosity; in her curiosity, a challenge.

Night appeared in little flecks on the under sides of leaves. Lily watched her grandfather. As twilight thickened, a similar shadow seemed to gather within him, behind his eyes. He was unnaturally pallid—a mere shell separating two shadows. One day it would crumble; his darkness would join that of night in the world. She would be alone, always alone, bodily alone...

Suddenly she thought of the stranger with security. What harm could he do her? How could she be harmed? She saw him quite distinctly, not in person, but as a separate outline as small as her hand, singing to itself, and an embodiment of sadness.

It pleased her now to add reasons to her instinctive decision not to share the secret. Her grandfather was old and not strong; he would not understand; it would only frighten him and remind him of his deafness. Now that it was too dark to sew, she folded the white cloths and laid them on the grass.

During that night she awoke and knew that the negro had come. As before, her body was already rigid, her heart-beats accelerated. On the floor around her bed the moonlight fell in crisp rectangles. Out of doors some trees rose from the lawn with dark columns, undecorated and abrupt. Between them the light clinked like a castanet.

The footsteps on the porch were undisguised and reckless. He fumbled at the screen-door, at the windows. He scratched the wire tentatively with another metal, and ceased as if afraid of the noise. Lily lifted herself in the bed upon her elbows. A deep sigh from without, sibilant against the teeth...

Her arms ached with tension. A great silence arose as a growing plant arises. Her imagination fixed upon it, half in terror, half in hope. It spread and shook out its leaves. In the garden a tree-toad tinkled to itself.

Lily slipped out of bed. Her nightgown swung about her ankles. As she crossed the moonlight her legs glimmered under the sheer cloth. A braid caught and slipped over the back of a chair. Her progress was slow and irregular as if she wavered or floated. Not a board protested under her bare feet, upraised at the instep. The pupils of her eyes were dilated for something not yet apparent, and she did not even glance at the chairs and tables between which she was moving.

The porch door thrust into the dark room a broad short blade of light. Lily skirted it, and saw the black man.

He was on the steps, his legs spread apart, his bare head bent so that his gaze rested in the gray grass. He wore tennis-shoes, trousers, no shirt, and a tight coat. Between its lapels the moonbeams rested on the close hard folds of his belly, like furrows turned by a chisel.

She had never seen a negro; separated from her by ten feet and a thin fabric of wire, he was not so black as her imagination had made him. In the dead brilliance his cheeks glimmered softly, pallid not in themselves but as a surface highly burnished. Only a film of color was on his lips. He rested his chin within hands almost white across the palms, and turned his great white eyes toward her. The damp curled upward around her bare body.

Midnight passed. The two poised there side by side. Awareness hung loosely, idly, in the dimness, the silver, the quiet; each of them had no reason but the other's presence to stay there, wide awake; but no accident altered their serene relation. The moon slipped through the sky. Sometimes the negro's sighs were clear; he seemed to be breathing forth some one mysterious vowel.

She brushed against a pillow, which fell and settled heavily on the floor. Surely he would hear and come! The blood rushed to her head in a loud flood.

But he did not. His desires, the tentacles thrust outward toward something in that house, had been withdrawn; and were gathered, in a knot almost visible, about some inner crisis. He rose abruptly, stretched himself, and strode away, over the grass. The dew plashed on his canvas shoes.

Before her grandfather came down stairs, Lily arose into a day lurid and insecure. Some robins worked upon the flagrant bright green sod. Everywhere were clots of color and vortices of movement she had never seen. A superb thunderhead palpitated in the sky like a tree with black blossoms.

These things drew her outdoors, but a smaller sight arrested her: upon the screendoor a gash three inches long, made by a wedge or chisel during that night. She stared at the opening, from which the soft wire bent back neatly.

The old man, whistling like a boy, found her there. He did not see the trace upon the door.

Prohibition

"O abstainer! do not ignore the pleas of
drunken men, but lead them back to the
tavern."

   –*The Arabian Nights*

VIII.

Prohibition

Old Riley lay, without hands or feet, on a red tapestry couch in the dirty sitting room, and blinked happily at the sunshine and at a bottle which stood in it beside him. An exceptionally hairy white dog crouched under his outstretched arm. All around him there were geraniums and begonias in rusty tin pails on dry-goods boxes. Through the window one could see little slatternly groves here and there, and a hill hollowed out on one side by a gravel pit like a great empty grave. Though no one asked him to, Old Riley sang a song. A child, standing as near the door as he could without being asked where he was going, stared reverently at the little drunkard, now crippled and famous and apparently happier than ever before.

Though the temperance movement had gained strength in that part of the country long before drink was prohibited by law, Old Riley was not the only notorious drunkard in the township. There was a farmer named Theodore Osten who was said to have broken off a bull's horns with his bare hands. He often pounded on the district schoolhouse door in the afternoon, demanded as many of his six children as were there, and took them whimpering home with him. Once he came back from the village with a butcher's knife in his hand. His wife escaped through the back yard, leaving her sixth baby behind. When she brought a crowd of the neighbors to rescue the child, he stuck somebody's hired man in the leg and, bursting into gloomy laughter, threw the knife at them all. But his wife would not be separated from him or let the neighbors have him sent to jail, and complained bitterly about the fines he was obliged to pay.

There was also the dreamy hired man, Charlie Fox, who got drunk chiefly in bad weather. He began to complain whenever clouds came up, but after five or six bottles of beer ceased to mind the elements. He would wander up and down in the worst blizzards, murmuring to anyone he met, "Hell of a storm we're having—suits me!" Or he would sit down in the mud outside a saloon window, his arms folded, his eyes shut, the rain streaming over his cheeks and under his wet wing-collar, the lamplight shining on his white, serene, weak face.

Even before the accident which had confined him to his bed, Old Riley had never been melancholy or dangerous. At his very worst he amused himself by letting young cattle out of pasture, by pushing over shocks of grain, chicken-coops, and beehives until he got tired. In spite of his practical jokes and his bad example to the young, the sober God-fearing farmers and their wives could not hate him at any time. The mingling of joy and catastrophe in his life confused even the most opinionated among them. They regarded him as something less than a man, an irresponsible animal in human form.

To their children, on the other hand, he always seemed more than human, and began to charm and frighten them even before he came into sight. Through the harvest fields at dusk they would hear a song coming toward them as if it were stumbling over the fields without a singer. Out of hollows or from the far side of hills, there would come the revolving thunder of his lumber-wagon wheels, the hiss and crack of the whip which he flourished like a long leather snake, and strangely melodious shouts—the shouts of a hunter or a jockey, the cries of a drunken hunter or a jockey on a wild horse. "Holy this" or "Holy that," he cried—this or that being one of those short words which mean more in sound to children than in sense to their elders. Children never had the courage to inquire about anything he did or said.

Dissipated happiness and a tragic accident... His happiness, while it lasted, was injurious to others and furnished the community with a token of its inner desperation, the inarticulate fields and farmhouses with an appalling voice. Disaster, when it overtook him, made him a symbol of every abnormal delight, of the durability of character, of contentment with catastrophe, and moreover saved his family from the consequences of his pleasures. Roistering joy on summer afternoons and evenings, a terrible event among deep snowdrifts, in the starlight... It is no wonder that the neighbors made no attempt to explain the meaning of Old Riley's story to their children, for a tragedy was its happy ending.

He usually went to a saloon in one of the adjacent villages about four o'clock in the afternoon. Sawing on the mouths of his nervous mares, he brought them to a standstill, clambered down from the high seat, gathered some flowers along the fence, tearing them up by the root, pinned them to the lid of his lamentable greasy cap with a nail, clambered back up, and started his team again with a good deal of shouting.

Some children on their way home from school, undaunted by his curses and his wild driving, climbed into the back of the lumber-wagon. Old Riley turned about and shouted, "Open yer mouths and shut yer eyes," and amused himself greatly by dropping pennies, nickels, and dimes into their mouths with one hand, cracking the whip over their heads with the other. When he missed his aim one youngster or another dropped to the ground instantaneously, like a little warrior picked off the vehicles by a sharpshooter, to spend the rest of the afternoon hunting the coins in the dust and gravel and among the nettles by the side of the road.

A few hours later, drunk enough and ready to go home, his pockets were empty. "I must 'a' give it all to the brats on the way," he explained to the bartender. "What a blasted fool I am! Now wouldn't ye know I'd do that. Ye know me anyway, Bill."

The bartender did know him: the next day or the day after he would deny his indebtedness; but his boys also knew their father and could be made to pay what was due—secretly, lest he give them a beating.

In his boyhood the eldest son, who was called Young Riley, had indeed followed his father into saloons in hope of getting him home sober. During this period the incorrigible man lost less of his money and did somewhat less damage to other people's property, but otherwise the youngster's presence put no restraint upon him. And he was fonder of his boys than of other men and liked to drink with them; so little by little, Young Riley and eventually the other son, Terrie, adopted the old man's ways. But Young Riley had certain principles, and would not leave the farm in the afternoon or permit his brother to do so; together they pretended to do the work in the fields which their father frivolously neglected.

All alone, therefore, in the early evening, Old Riley started home, too drunk to care when he arrived. He saw the open gate of a neighbor's barnyard and swung through it, shouting and flourishing his black-snake whip. He tied the team to a heavy pig trough, but they pulled it along the ground until they could eat from a haystack.

As he entered the warm stable where men were milking, boys and little girls throwing down corn fodder and feeding the calves, Old Riley swayed and bowed ceremoniously. In his hand he was carrying a length of wild grapevine in blossom, and he knotted it under his chin like a necktie. "Gad," he said, "wild grapes smell like a snake."

A small boy who heard him say this spent much of his time in hunting the delicate, brilliant grass-snakes, and resolved to kill another tomorrow to find out how it smelled.

Then Old Riley sat down on a milk-stool and gave an account of what had happened to him lately, boasting and putting on airs and reciting in conclusion a long list of curse words, softly, rather mechanically, like a priest telling his beads. He nodded his head as old hens do when they have a certain sickness and kept on shaking his fist in the air while his tired body sagged lower and lower, lurching a little from side to side. He fell off the milk-stool;

and there at last he lay, on a pile of clean straw for bedding the animals, taking a short nap, the one belligerent arm still raised above him.

The farmer and his young hired men, laughing uneasily, went on with their work. They also might have taken to drink; this was the moral lesson of the ridiculous. The youngsters were enchanted, as if the old fellow were a small dancing bear or the monkey of an invisible organ-grinder whose music only they could hear; and they gazed at him with starry, disgusted, incredulous eyes—the admirable eyes of children born and bred in the country.

He was tolerated thus in the evening in the barns even of his most self-respecting neighbors because, when all was said and done, he did no harm. Not, at least, to anyone but his own flesh and blood, wife and children, and that was the sort of harm which seemed appropriate to them, or which they deserved. The worst gossips in the community said, "They're all kind o' heartless, those Rileys. Heaven knows what could happen to make such as them unhappy"; and their faces lighted up as if they had discovered a recipe for simplifying life: some people have no hearts to break... Perhaps they found Old Riley sympathetic because he had as little patience with human disappointments as they.

So when he had rested and cheered himself by the seeming benevolence of one neighbor or another, he would set out again, disputing with himself as he untied his horses whether he was hungrier than he was thirsty; his thirst was never altogether quenched, but it was always hunger which brought him home. He remembered that he had forgotten the groceries he had promised his wife to buy, and the money she had given him was gone. She would upbraid him; he would probably have to beat her to put her in the wrong.

May Riley was a pleasant, shiftless woman who had been frightened for so many years that she had begun to seem a little weak in her mind. People believed that he did not actually hurt her; at any rate, she hid her face in her skirts without crying out, and never whimpered or showed any bruises after it was over. But she gave her entire time to shivering anticipation of his next drunken return from the village, and so neglected her housework, cooked badly, and wore her dresses, petticoats, and shawls in mere tatters wound around her loose-jointed body. Sometimes it was because she cooked badly that he abused her, at others because she was not as pretty as she had been on their wedding day. In those days, years before, she had looked like their daughter Angeline. Her brothers called her Candy on account of her hair, which hung in curls the color of taffy all around her pretty, pale face.

Driving home through the bland summer evening, Old Riley meditated on the weather or the landscape or the poor farms he passed. The weather was an entertainment, the landscape never seemed tedious, the farmhouses never mean and melancholy—because he was always drunk. Alcohol saved him from the mediocrity of the world.

His younger son, Terence or Terrie, the lovable Riley, was like him in this respect. He also drank for fun, and being drunk was an enchantment; then even the banal saloons, the poor farmers' women with dirty hair and sagging bodies who knew only too well how to take care of themselves, the lonely sheds and stables took on a bright and distorted appearance. But unlike his father, he could not be drunk all the time. His brother, for the pleasure of governing him, allowed him little money to spend, little time to make love to such women as there were; and he dreamed of a life which would have that shining, deformed appearance even in broad daylight when he was sober. He wanted to join the navy, talking to others and even to himself about the places where the battleship would probably stop—the shore of the sea covered with odd buildings, the hundreds of sailors as good but no better than he, the welcoming women crying out and agitating their shawls… What a wild life he would lead in those places, buying what he liked, fed and clothed like a child by the government! He thought it would be the most agreeable thing in the world, and perhaps he was not wrong.

Driving home, sitting up very straight and gesturing with the whip or the long reins as if the road were lined with people with their eyes fixed on him, Old Riley thought of a quarrel he had been engaged in. A great anger arose in his heart and, forgetting the quarrel in the storm of his emotion, he searched his mind for another pretext, an object or person upon whom it might be spent. If his sons were arguing about the navy when he got home, he would thrash them and they would see…

For Young Riley would not let his brother enlist, indeed threatened to kill him if he did—perhaps out of jealous affection, perhaps in dread of the tedium of his own experience if he were left alone. Nor would he go away with the boy, somehow unwilling to leave the scene of an honest, laborious life, though not leading it or likely to. He was ashamed of keeping Terrie back, but as long as he suffered from alcoholic stomach trouble could make no sacrifices; blamed everything, including his own selfishness, on their father; and turned for forgetfulness to the very cup which he wanted to forget. Drunk or sober, when his anger arose it confused him about everything.

It wore itself out like any other forbidden passion, and was succeeded by a heavy anxiety and a sense of guilt. He had no right to blame his father and brother; he was equally good for nothing; but he had too much common sense to be so cheerful about the results of their dissipation. The farm had been mortgaged twice; no one knew what would happen to the old people if it came to a foreclosure; and Young Riley, especially in the early morning after a night's drinking, thought desperately about the future.

Old Riley did not. He brooded, as he drove home, upon a stupendous lie that he was preparing to tell, a song that he might sing or was singing. Though to his regret he had no bottle in his pocket, he seemed to be getting more and more drunk and was not sure that he knew the road home; it did not matter, his horses knew. And in a vague way he foresaw that he would be surprised to find his wife and children in the house that could scarcely be called his home, though he had been born in it, and looked forward with vague pleasure to falling upon them in instantaneous fury, and chasing one or another outdoors or indoors, and spoiling all their plans.

In and about that house there was an atmosphere of slatternly grace and peace until he came. Neglect had contributed to the ordinary building and the barn and sheds its ramshackle beauty, the great comfort of idle men. The gables were sway-backed, the weathervane twisted; the barn doors hung from one hinge apiece; the half-wild fowls had learned to fly up on the rotten branches; and two or three sheep that were left of a large flock lay at the doorstep with the dogs. The moon was coming up and filled the yard with liquid brightness and clean shadows tossed about by the weeds and the grass. All about stood slim poplars whose little branches hung down in rows of curls as perfect as Angeline's. The soft moon rose higher, stirred up new odors, warmed the dew. The balm, the dust, the summer drifting down, clouded the faces of May Riley and her children.

The old woman crouched on the doorstep, asleep, with her fists full of goose feathers she was sorting to put in a pillow. A little way away, on a dry-goods box, her sons sat close together, with a whiskey bottle on the ground within reach. They had a large accordion which each played in turn, the other singing, or even, with a good deal of laughter, both playing at once—one large ruddy hand fingering the keys, one manipulating the bellows out of which some of the air escaped with a sigh.

Angeline was hiding in the haymow with her beau. It had always been the same one, a young man named Andie Roy. He had been going with her less of late, or seemed, at least, to be less serious in his intentions. Angeline blamed her father and brothers and determined to have him, in spite of their bad reputation, in spite of his scruples. They hid in the haymow now, because Andie was pretending to be afraid of Young Riley, who knew, of course, that he was there—actually because he was trying to be there without thinking of it himself, having made up his mind not to come.

At a pause in the music the brothers, hearing their whispers and laughter, shook their fists in that direction and winked at each other. Then the throbbing of music ran out again in the blood-heat of the air, far out, their unskilled, heavy, palpitating voices joining it now and then. Over the drowsy countryside these sounds troubled young girls lying ill at ease, and reawakened the ambitions, the shames and grievances, the homesickness for places unseen, of boys more finely bred than the Rileys, and set overworked mothers weeping for dead children. But in the Irish yard there was no sadness in the music or in anything else: Terrie had forgotten the navy for the moment; his brother had forgotten the mortgages, was neither drunk nor sober, and did not care; the mother was asleep; Angeline was in her young man's arms; and they all enjoyed the music and the time of night as if there were no past or future.

Then the lumber-wagon rolled into the yard. Old Riley clambered down, threw the reins on the ground, shouted a few curses, picked up a good-sized stick, and strode into the midst of his family. He made a lunge at the boys with the stick. They took refuge in the wagon-shed, knowing that their father, in his condition, would not be able to find his way in the dark among the wheels and thills and harness lying about. The accordion sank to the ground and cried one hopeless note like a dying swan's as the breath went out of it and it collapsed. The whiskey bottle tipped over, the whiskey gurgled out, the dry earth drank it up.

Then the old man turned his attention to his wife, shaking out the bag of goose feathers in her face. She woke in a sort of little winter of its contents, and at first did not know where she was. just as he was about to strike her for her complaints, his sons, from the shadow of the house, jumped on his back, and tied his hands and feet with some pieces of rope. He roared and his wife wept, and then he began to sing a song. The boys squatted at his feet in menacing attitudes, but they listened to the song, and it was evident that they loved him.

Angeline came out of the barn into the moonlight, rubbing her forehead where the curls caressed it. Terrie shouted, "Where's your beau, Candy?"

"He ain't been here, has he?" she answered craftily. "l been asleep. What's the matter with pa?"

"You're a liar," the boys said, "but wha' do we care?"

Andie Roy was not there then. At the first of her father's shouts the girl had whispered to him, "You better skip, there's trouble." He had slid down out of the haymow, mistaken a trap-door for the ladder into the stable, and landed heavily on a pile of hay in the bull's manger. The little old bull, which smelled like a lion, had snuffled him, and he got up and hurried out through the barnyard.

Andie Roy was so much excited and so much in love that he wondered if he were going to die, and there was pain in several parts of his body. So he lay down by the side of the road and, for a while, cried like a small boy, pressing his mouth against the knuckles of his fists. It seemed to be one of the greatest sorrows in the world that night. The night grew more and more fair. The tree over his head dropped now and then a burned or withered leaf. The lovelier the weather the more the boy suffered from his feelings about Angeline, which seemed to lead nowhere.

His widowed mother and the Catholic priest, Father Hoyle, had encouraged his determination not to marry her. Father Hoyle said over and again that Andie was one of the most superior boys in his parish, so he ought not to mix with disobedient riffraff like the Rileys. He was particularly anxious that his young men should not drink, since the Protestants favored prohibition and made the excesses of the Irish Catholics both a political and a doctrinal issue. Andie knew that he was inclined to liquor and that Terrie and Young Riley had too much power over him.

During the spring of that year, having loitered in a saloon with those two, he had been going down a lane which led through one corner of a woods. And a voice had said to him, "Andrew, Andrew — get you!" He had been infinitely moved and frightened, not so much by the sound of the voice which had been no more alarming than that of a tom-cat or a hoot-owl or anything else one may hear when one has had too much to drink, as by the meaning of what it said in relation to the bad company he had been keeping, his temptations, his mother's grievances.

He had told Father Hoyle about it, and the superstitious old man, not knowing what to believe himself and hoping for a matter-of-fact explanation, had repeated the story to a number of parishioners. Thereafter when Andie saw the two Rileys, out with girls or in a saloon, they had shouted at him, "Andrew, Andrew—get you!" If they got him he would be as bad as they were. His mother had assured him that if he did not reform, their little farm would have to be mortgaged before long, and he would probably beat her, and they would be looked down upon by everybody. So Andie had told Father Hoyle that he meant to give no more thought to Angeline Riley.

The old priest had said, "Now if ye don't mean to marry the girl, keep away from there. I know what you young Irish are. There's the Old Nick in yuh."

Andie had tried to keep away, but a sort of fixed idea of Candy's pale yellow curls and her eyes of a melted, diluted blue tempted him back in the evening very often. He had tried to persuade himself that he was getting over it by degrees, but he was not. Instead, his disapproval of her family was wearing away; he was beginning to enjoy their kind of happiness. But for his mother he would not have hesitated to go with the girl into another township and get married before another priest. He did not dare to try to seduce her, and she would not let him go any farther than so far, fearing that he would cease to care for her as soon as he had had his own way. That was a good thing, for he would have cared all the more and cared too much as it was.

So as he went back home from her house he shed tears, gnawed at the back of his hand, and even cursed a little.

He stopped his sniffling just in time, for his mother was leaning over the garden fence in the moonlight, and like an echo she began to cry where he had left off. "You don't look at things right. You been off havin' a good time with those wild Rileys, and little you think whether I've been here cryin' my eyes out or not."

Before he went to bed Andie spent an hour defending the Rileys and trying to prove that he had a right to marry whomever he liked, though he realized that there was not a particle of honesty in what he said, for at bottom his mother and he were always of the same opinion. Since he could not free his heart or change his mind, matters went from bad to worse for him the rest of the summer and all fall.

The Rileys also began to look at the seamy side of things. The man who held the mortgages would give them only until spring, and obviously money could not be raised during the winter. May began to fail in health. Terrie told his sister, "I guess Bud is getting funny in his head"; by which he meant that Young Riley was growing infinitely sad and bad-tempered. Terrie himself grew more and more sullen about the navy; on one occasion he struck his mother, and his father and brother took turns punishing him. Angeline lost hope of getting Andie to marry her. They all grew older and looked faded. Only Old Riley never changed in appearance or behavior—he seemed immortal.

The winter set in early, frosting the corn before it was ripe and spoiling good pasture, as if to make sure that they should be unable to meet the mortgage. Old Riley had to begin to sell the pigs and cows as money was needed for food and drink.

There was a heavy fall of snow just before Christmas, and at that time a special election was held in Belleville. Riley left home with his boys right after the noonday meal, Young Riley and Terrie with the bobsleigh and the team, he himself following alone in the cutter. They always made of any political occasion a carnival of drinking.

Under the sleigh runners the crisp snow made a loud chirruping; the sleigh bells left behind them in the air their flurry of jangling notes. Around the muzzles of the horses and the mouths of the men the breath floated like visible souls about to vanish. Where there had been masses of living flowers, there lay a vast garden of dead, white and blue-white—the wind having twisted the tops of all the snow-banks into bloom.

In Belleville the Rileys established themselves at Schimmel's saloon, the one nearest the town hall. The boys began by playing cards, and earned a good many drinks. The men of the country came in before or after voting; since it was bitterly cold, all drank more than usual for the warmth. Old Riley wedged himself between a barrel and the bar so that he did not have to depend entirely on his legs, and there made eloquent speeches for all the factions in turn, tossing off the rewards of his eloquence.

Smoke, hanging in warm layers, blotted out the eyes or hands or mouths of men on the other side of the room, and mixed in a vague sparkle the shining of varnished wood, glasses, lighted matches. Outside, the temperature fell below zero. Men shuddered when it came time to go; the Rileys felt fortunate to be too drunk to have to think of it. They ate some sausages from the bar and let the time pass. At last they were alone in the foul, clouded, warm place amid the debris of refreshment, fatigue, argument; and the bar-keeper wanted to go to bed.

So, cursing and stumbling about in their sheepskin coats, they went down to the stables over the crunching snow, over the frosted filth, and through the stiff, echoing cold. The boys were engaged in another argument about the navy and hitched up their horses without paying any attention to the old man, expecting him to follow them with his cutter. But instead he rolled into the back of their bobsleigh and fell asleep there before they drove out of the yard.

There were dazzling stars. The snowdrifts over the land looked like innumerable ghosts lying side by side. Terrie and Young Riley were angry with each other; but after all, it was an arctic night and they were young and warm, so they drew close together under the blankets and ceased to argue.

Behind them their father did not snore because he was lying face down in the straw, and they did not discover him. The road rose in a hump over every drift that had been blown up; the sleigh lifted on the crest, lurched into the trough, of wave after wave of snow.

About half way home, Old Riley rolled out in the road. Perhaps he did not wake up; at least he was not sufficiently sobered by the fall to shout or to rise and follow his boys on foot.

The next day at dawn the first farmer on that road to go to the cheese factory found him there and brought him home. The doctor who was called in found it necessary to remove his feet at the ankles and his hands at the wrist.

In due time it became evident that it was a happy ending for them all. His wife was no longer afraid of him, and became a quite capable woman. The effort of ministering to his pain until the amputations healed and of clothing and feeding him and giving him drink roused her from her apathy of years—years of waiting at home to be abused.

Shaken to the bottom of his sluggish heart, Young Riley had no difficulty now in ceasing to drink. He went to a Ladies' Aid supper at the Methodist Church, stole a temperance pledge, signed it without telling anyone, and kept it hidden in his bedroom. Refreshed by disaster, his fleshy face, once inanimate and middle-aged with gloom, lighted up. To all intents and purposes he had inherited the farm, and he would make it profitable. The banker who owned the mortgages was persuaded to give them another year to begin paying their debts.

Young Riley was glad to let his brother go away somewhere to make a fresh start in life. So Terrie joined the navy in the spring, and sent home picture postal cards from Villefranche, Cardiff, and Kiel.

Since the Rileys were a changed family, there was nothing to keep Angeline and Andie apart. They were married and were happy in the most ordinary way in the world. In a little less than due time a child was born; they named it after Old Riley, whose given name had been forgotten for years.

The prohibition law was passed. Some of Old Riley's temperance neighbors, greatly elated, wanted to ask him what he thought of that. They found the little mutilated man who had been the terror of the community lying in a bay-window, and forgot what they had come for. The room was filled with an atmosphere of patience, indolence, and lawlessness. Sword ferns, begonias, and radiant geraniums stood all about his couch. Over his head one could see out over the countryside, and there was a hill hollowed out like the grave of a giant who has come to life, dug himself up, and wandered away. A child who had followed the neighbors in, shrank in awe toward the door, shrank from the little man's evident felicity. For he was drunk, though he had been punished by a divine law against it and though a law on earth had been passed. His arms came to an end inside his sleeves, his legs inside his tattered trouser-legs. He seemed to enjoy the scrutiny due him as an object lesson and not to care what the moral was. His smiling wife went on giving him whiskey, setting the glass with a straw in it on a chair within reach of his mouth.

The Sailor

To Mary Reynolds

IX.

The Sailor

Terence or Terrie Riley, back from sea, leaned on the edge of the water-trough in the barnyard. His brother beside him, with a hog-crate for a table, was mending harness. Terrie could have helped him, but as if to suggest that having come home he would not stay, did nothing. A cigarette was always fuming in one of his heavy hands, the other was tucked under his belt. His almond finger nails were outlined with tar. On the back of the fingers at the ring-joint had been tattooed in blue ink, a letter to a finger: HOLD FAST.

His brother's country eyes rested now and then on these two animated words which could not be washed away, but he would not make any inquiry concerning them. Neither did he comment on the less definite alterations in the sailor's appearance. He wore, for example, a belt instead of suspenders, and wore it about his hips rather than his waist. His body thus elongated, if he stood on one leg, curved out loosely in the opposite direction. If he stood erect he held the initialled hands close to his sides like someone always about to begin a dance. His eyes looked even bluer now that the eyelids were coarsened and ruddy. His mouth had hardened into an expression; once it had been like a sturdy girl's, in spite of the drink. He still had curly hair the color of bee's-wax and pointed teeth which seemed to bite his tongue when he smiled. It seemed sinister to his brother that he laughed less and smiled more.

The elder Riley had fancied that the sea was a hard place and that sailors were rude, bow-legged creatures, perhaps dark as a result of storms and salt, perhaps tongue-tied from perpetual solitude. So he was astonished by this merely flushed and tired home-comer, in whose face instead of age there was a look of strange precocity—knots of worn muscle, soft shadows of grimaces left by foreign emotions—indifferent to all that he had left behind several years before, voluble as an aged man.

In spite of his talkativeness, he was somehow inexpressive. He was not thinking in the words he used or, for that matter, in any words. He repeated himself, uttered sentences in which there was nothing remarkable very emphatically, and combined the weakest phrases with the coarsest ejaculations, as if to give his past actions a virility which his ideas did not have, about which he might even have had certain doubts. Meanwhile his eyes lost their precision, and he seemed to be gazing at the very fruits of experience, with the bloom still upon them, his greed unsatisfied.

The sky was burning all about the big Wisconsin sun. Hogs sighed in the mud-hole behind the straw-stack. There were no human beings to be seen in any field.

"It was just luck to get sent on the other side," Terrie said. "They work 'em hard in the Pacific, they tell me. We got around a lot. Brest and Cardiff and Kiel and Marseilles and all those places. Where I liked it best was Villefranche."

He was never going back there again, it had made him miserable, he loathed it yet liked it best; and he thought of the little boys on the water-front with wet-looking eyes, cigarette butts, dirty habits, some of them blond, supposed to be American, sailors having got ignorant or merely scheming girls into trouble. He wished he had done so, to have left a baby there like him, but he guessed his girl Zizi and her friend Minette would not want to be bothered with one—neither would he, in their place.

A young steer came down the lane to drink from the trough. Its hide kept rippling under a swarm of flies. It sighed with its plump, emasculate muzzle under water. The water was dark and there were vivid lumps of slime in it.

"Yeah, I liked Villefranche all right. A good town, but awful dirty."

A little half-moon of stone-and-plaster town in a narrow-necked harbor, all the buildings facing the sea, flesh-pink and yellow like a faded canary-bird and different shades of white with blue shutters; all one cliff of tenements, a street which was a staircase crossing at right angles another which was a filthy tunnel; around little squares the walls painted with false windows and false half-open or closed shutters and ornaments in false relief, like opera settings of canvas seeming to hang diagonally overhead, seeming to sway because of the brightness of the air; with a constant festivity of washing on strings from window to window, worn-out banners and ragged flags of underwear, with glimpses of dishevelled beds, and shapeless females leaning out of the upper stories with their dresses slipping off their shoulders; and all the ground floors breathing forth an odor of the saliva of a vast beast. Above the tenements a church which looked like a tombstone and higher up, in walled gardens, the villas, bright and ugly and muffled in spectral vegetation—instead of moist lawns and trees a stiff plumage of palms and other palms shaped like pineapples and cactus with its big blades of paralyzed grass and the nervous, translucent olive-orchards; and still higher up, insignificant mountains of stones and stone-pines, without peaks, without snow, without color, looking dried-up in the diamond light. A landscape wisely spoiled for the sake of the people; down below in the port the young women harmed whenever the men enjoyed it (when Terrie first came there he could not bear to see women crying and gave them anything to stop it) and nothing done to the men, little or nothing required of them—a peaceful, immoral liberty left to do its work for good or ill. The air was always scented; added to the different odors of the sea there were roses and lilies, orange blossoms and carnations, in a mixture; one morning one of these would fade out of the potpourri and another take its place; you never knew which was which, you never spoke of it, most of the time you did not smell it at all, tirelessly breathing instead the odor given off along the quay by the row of bars—an acrid compound of sweat, stale liquor, cheaply perfumed girls, sour mops, bad breath—the odor exhaled in furnished rooms by love and sleep.

"It's a small town, but you could raise hell," Terrie Riley told his brother, back in Wisconsin. "They don't have any winter. There's quite a good-sized city near, too."

The wages of a common sailor in francs were the equivalent of a rich young Frenchman's allowance; if his record and his health were good he was entitled to every other night on shore, and the work on board was easy, like sleep a chance to sober up and a regular refreshment of desire; all of which wealth of time and money and vitality was spent in the neighboring great city on complicated amusements that they simplified to suit their tastes, or right there in the sight of the battleship, in the Villefranche bars, their back walls jewelled with bottles, a coughing music from the tin morning-glories of old-fashioned phonographs in most of them; only the "Home Hotel" bar (the headquarters of the flock of women who followed the navy from port to port) had an orchestra: a tuberculous girl violinist, a very muscular pianist, a drummer like a rat with a diagonal mouth and no hair.

In Wisconsin an old horse came down to the trough in its turn, the hide of its shoulders worn out, its bones making their way out and up through the flesh. It stood between the two brothers, and for a moment one of its sagging, gelatinous eyes rested on Terrie's face. Certainly he was no farmer any more; animals made him vaguely uncomfortable, though he had learned that it was not when human beings were like animals that they were most terrible or dangerous.

He remembered the great orgy at Mother Seraphine's the night before the ship left for home, the last night he spent with his girl Zizi whom he thought he loved and was glad to get rid of. The sailors bought hard-boiled eggs by the dozen to throw at each other; one danced with a full bottle balanced in his mouth, the brandy streaming down his neck and all over his uniform; some, as close together as they could get in a corner, tried to sing, but were choked by who could tell what vague emotion; some danced and fell down, but would not fall alone; through the air, smoky like an olive-tree, you could see a mix-up of the ecstasy of faces, of limp knees, of the admirable gestures of drunken hands, vaguely keeping time with several hoarse banjos; suddenly with a shattering of glass a grinning man made his entrance through a high window, having climbed up on the grape-arbor, and Mother Seraphine's fat husband, beside himself, ran around in circles, but smiled, able to afford to smile. The women were sad, especially the youngest, and preferred to sit in corners, though the one they called Tata held on to two sailors and her old hair which was like hay came down—it was she who sold dope. Terrie's girl Zizi had some bills in her stocking and counted them impassively; she had made a fool of him, but he could afford to be tender because he was never going to see her again and besides he was too drunk to know the difference between enemy and friend—no one was his enemy, no one was his friend. The sea, like a bird or a jewel in the daytime, had turned black that night; there was nothing left of the battleship but some sparkling balconies up in the dark and a sparkling staircase leading from nowhere to nowhere, or in fact from Villefranche to Wisconsin; and Terrie was going to take away with him the lesson of the former without quite knowing what it was.

"The only trouble with Villefranche was: there were too many women," he told his brother. "There was one they called the Folle. That means, the Nut."

She had married an American sergeant who was killed in the war and drew a pension from the government, so she was well-to-do; she was still young and healthy; she followed the ships but did not care for the men, followed the women; she wore her hat wrong side before or two skirts, one over and higher than the other, and imagined that she started all the fashions; the girls often got her to dance with Zizi, who whirled her around until she had a fit of hysterics, at which everyone laughed, but it was not cruel because she enjoyed it; and late at night she walked up and down the quay singing operas that she made up as she went along, a symbol of abnormal ways of passing the time, agitating a ghostly shawl.

Pressed down in one corner of the Wisconsin landscape between the sunshine and the monotonous fields there was a mass of clouds full of spasmodic thunder — anger about to break, a humiliating story untold. Probably it was going to rain.

Terrie could have gone on all afternoon telling anecdotes about women, but his brother did not seem particularly interested. There was a girl who came down from Paris in the height of fashion, a white turtle-necked sweater with a string of pearl beads over it and a little dog on a leash; she played cards with the men, lost all her money one night, and had no room; she had cheated at poker, so they did nothing but laugh at her, and she paced up and down the quay, sobbing as loudly as she could, "Where'm I going to sleep? Where'm I going to sleep?" Then a big sailor from Kansas swung down the staircase street, and not knowing what was the matter, walked up to her, said, "Aw shut up! You make too much noise," slapped her face, and got into the launch going to the ship; the girl staggered back against the wall, too astonished to fight back, then whimpered with a disturbing, soft simplicity, and finally went off somewhere.

As far as one could see in Wisconsin that afternoon, trees were rolling in their deep valley beds, and there was an atmosphere of sorrow which nothing had happened to cause.

Fleshy, serene women, heartsick girls making a violent effort to amuse, others hungry and fantastic, some rosy with fever as well as rouge, adolescent beggars making exciting equivocal appeals for pity, old spent saleswomen, all with the happy look of intoxicated sterility... There was one, almost a child, with the protruding mouth and fine glazed eyes of an alley cat, Terrie forgot her name; there was one who wore glasses and looked like a school-teacher; there was Minette, Zizi's friend, a pallid beast who never slept.

Along the Wisconsin road passed two hired girls in gingham aprons. Their cool faces with a mingled expression of fear and independence meant nothing to the returned sailor. In spite of their youth, their long bodies already looked hollow, like those of mothers after childbirth…

Whereas the women abroad were short-legged and rounded out, even the thin ones; their glances were both brazen and dependent; around their eyes the eyelids were ashen; the moistly painted mouths were hard in the middle and broken in the corners; they did not walk like men; and even their dishonesty, their anger, were flattery of a sort.

There were two Turks, one vigorous and handsome, the other enormously fat but more popular, especially with the older sailors, who spoke a little English and no French, having taken off the veil to follow the ships, and late at night the vigorous one, tying about her a shawl with fringes, often gave an exhibition of their dances, turning all the middle of her body as if it were a wheel, jerking her neck almost out of joint rhythmically, drumming softly with one index finger against the other over her head, Pauline, her friend, grovelling at her feet with the glittering nickel tray on which drinks were served; and a certain sailor in his excitement covered his eyes, whimpered, and cried aloud, "Ooh, take her away…"

"I took turns with most of 'em," Terrie boasted without enthusiasm to his brother. "Then after a while I got to playing around steady with a girl from there. That was Zizi. One was enough for me, I figured. And she was healthy and kind'a steady. She didn't cost much. She was a good kid in a lot'a ways."

Once an adolescent girl of a miserable Algerian family who wanted to have sweethearts and better clothes and whose mother beat her, was driven down the street by one of her young brothers, and took refuge in a bar, among the women; an unlovely little animal, she sobbed and beat her forehead with her dark fists; the sailors bought her sandwiches, the women petted her; she wanted to return home but was afraid, and it was Zizi who had the courage to go with her to the one-room home in the underground street, hoping to conciliate the Mohammedans; but they gave her a black eye before they began to punish the girl.

When she came back, shedding tears but trying to laugh, she and Terrie went to a quieter place, a green-painted café under an arbor of wistaria, empty but for two Filipinos, cooks on board, playing checkers; over the zinc bar there was a framed poster of a woman with blushing breasts and violets in her hair, a sort of patron saint; and there Zizi sat, wistful at the right moment, smoking, the smoke curling up over her tempting tired mouth, holding his hand; and later, in her poor room, she was like a little fern, moist and colorless, motionless but opening.

"I got real crazy about her," Terrie told his brother. "Crazy, I tell you."

The mimosa was in bloom, clinging branches dipped in a sweet yellow snuff, its odor tickling the throat with a mysterious thirst; and in the morning on the quay of slabs of stone, where some of the fishing-nets dried like splashes of sepia applied with a brush while old women mended the others, the girls of the bar were lazy and restless, preening themselves. In the evening the sea slept, and when the moon rose the villas and roads and precipices lay in complete reflections on the surface of the harbor; and in her little room where Zizi lay in a torn pink blanket, by moonlight, by street-lamp light, by the sparkle of the lighthouse, her body was now snowy, now gray as a pearl, and all was perfect. She caressed him from head to foot, mechanically, carefully, like a cat with its kitten. He could not make her laugh, and as the night passed and he grew quite sober a sort of meek and pure delirium took command; yet this woman was no novelty to him, there was no novelty in women… He wanted her in the very moment of possession, wanted her not there but in Wisconsin, felt homesick for the farm and the snow. When he went back to the ship early in the morning it was misty and soundless, and there in the harbor with Cap Ferrat's arm around it, floated the battleship like an insane silver-gray palace; he was grateful to it for having brought him there, thought how he had made fun of other sailors who had married or wanted to marry their girls in port, and thought that he had not known what he was talking about.

Terrie would have liked to explain to his brother how and why he had considered marrying this French girl. But it had come to nothing in the end. So he kept it to himself.

He told Zizi that if she behaved well he would marry her at the end of the year and take her to America, whereupon she clenched her fists excitedly as if the promise were a sumptuous gift, but only for a moment; then gazed out to sea with a sort of patient grimace, not deigning to believe good news; but after that loved him with a new vitality—systematic, oppressive, interested—which hurt and excited him still more; an extreme jealousy was added to his pleasure, he saying "You're my woman, see," the girl weeping sincerely; so in the tumult of drinks and rendezvous, appetites and punishments, friends in trouble, money lost or stolen, fights and dancing, weeks of their quiet, heedless, bitter idyll passed. Then, of course, the battleship went on to other ports; Zizi stayed there and he sent her money every month; meanwhile his relative continence was just another kind of sensuality, and he exasperated his friends by his sentimental bad temper.

"When we got back there my girl had a girl-friend they called Minette, the bastard. She was all right at first."

He could remember the day he met her, a plump, white, older woman with gleaming eyes and a drooping pink mouth who stood beside Zizi in the square behind the hotel in front of a butcher shop with bead portières to keep out the flies, a pile of livers on a table upheld by an iron Cupid painted red. What could have been said with so little of two languages in common? So he put his arm around Zizi and mechanically caressed her, while the other stared at him shamelessly and licked her lips, and he felt a delicious uneasiness because Zizi did not seem jealous.

"She was a bad one, that Minette," he insisted to his brother, who went on working without a sign of being impressed. His eyes swept the scene in Wisconsin with irregular glances. There was a difference between his eyes and his brother's, which had the appearance of astigmatism that serenity and fatigue and long vistas make common among farmers. Terrie's were charged with nervous apathy, the apathy of appetites that have outlived desire, of satiety that is still sensitive. Essentially it was this difference which he needed to explain and could not.

In the afternoon, somewhat drunk, he went up to Zizi's room, found the two girls on the couch in each other's arms apparently reading a newspaper, and felt something which resembled a high fever before he had had time to shut the door behind him — the new girl rich and pale, as if bloodless, with shadows of dimples here and there, and dark willowy familiar Zizi; clumsily he forced his way between them, for a moment preferred the blonde, and there was a barbaric luxury in the poor room which he understood then only as one more indulgence to the male among women, the sailor on shore, feeling shame for the first time and liking it. Presently he kept quiet, having had just enough drink neither to sleep soundly nor to stay wide awake; it was hard to focus his attention on certain sounds which he heard, certain movements which he felt, but they made him think himself somehow neglected in his drowsiness, and when he opened his eyes he had to look at the two girls a long time before he saw what he saw: an embrace which had more desperation and gentleness than any he had ever taken part in; their eyes were closed, he might as well not have been there; he closed his eyes, pretended to be fast asleep; and it was if there were around the middle of his body a great ribbon of girls' bodies tied with the knot of a kiss, the bow-knot — not his kiss.

"Zizi didn't give a damn for me after that," he told his brother. "She was crazy about her."

Later, looking back, he seemed to have made a fatal discovery that afternoon, but it could not have been then, for he had been happy and pleased with Zizi, thinking that everything was meant for his pleasure; but in a few days the enjoyment turned to cynicism, and cynicism to a sickly sense of frustration, thorough and instructive frustration; for the girls' subsequent behavior revealed that sensuality, its stranglehold of one person upon another, was stronger in proportion as it was inapt to be satisfied; what was the good then of being a strong man, a young sailor …

"She and that Minette played a lot'a dirty tricks on me after that."

His reason to be proud of himself had been taken away, it was a kind of emasculation; the two girls preyed upon this sudden lack of character, this new sophistication which tormented him as if it were his vice, and treated him more and more badly in order to get paid, in dollars, to stop; Zizi would no longer understand what he said or speak the little English that she knew, and Minette's hatred was made perfectly clear, for she lied to the sailors who were his best friends and got him into fights; and they locked him out of Zizi's room which he paid for, only to lead him back in triumph between them the next day, not only drunk but vindictive, hoping his desires would do them harm, not only morose but weak.

"Every time I went with Zizi she stole my money out'a my pants and gave it to the girlfriend to buy snow. She never stole nothin' before."

"What's that, snow?" the elder brother asked.

"Coke. It's a kind of snuff. They get lit up on it."

Then, when he wanted only to get away, Zizi persecuted him with his former promise to marry her; she cried, without losing hope, and for the first time in his life he took pleasure in another's weeping, in consoling another for the lack of what it was in his power to give; thus, bit by bit, he had become civilized, like a foreigner; but the battleship was going home, his time as a sailor was up, and he thought then that he would be glad to get back to Wisconsin.

Unable to say any more to his brother about Zizi, he said, "It ain't no fighting fleet they send over there. Just for show. Old boats, rotten guns. They'd have to drag 'em up on land if the' was any war. Just advertisement."

And in fact the foreigners were impressed; it proved that America was rich, that all Americans had fine bodies, were clean and well-dressed, and under favorable circumstances could stand any amount of regular debauchery. Terrie had been one of a great many ambassadors—ambassadors to Europe's fallen women at least, learning incidentally what "fallen" meant; and it was his brother, the pathetically hardy, sullen, and industrious farmer with a great hulk of a body incapable of most pleasures, whom they had been sent abroad to represent, and having done so they could not be what he was any more; figures in a drunken, superb, idle parade who must fall out of line after a certain number of years, and be out of a job and out of touch with everything...

His brother put aside his work on the harnesses and went up into the barn to throw down fodder for the bull and the horses which were not let out to pasture. Terrie followed him, loquacious still because he had not said what he wanted to say.

"They gave us a great send-off the night we left. Something to remember, I tell you. And the night before."

Thus his thought returned to his girl; the night before they left, the night of the orgy at Mother Seraphine's, she had stood for a moment outside, on a slab of stone at the water's edge, looking back through the open door where her friend Minette was laughing and stumbling to the music with one arm around a sailor and the other around a young man of the town; and she had a strange expression both of hate and sympathy, an expression which seemed to affirm that she was the one who was neglected and betrayed, but her face had not looked living at all: like that of a stone statue amid the excess, the malice, the happiness, like the sculpture of a dried-up fountain he had seen in a crowded street somewhere over there—dried-up for him at least.

The next day all the women wept, which flattered and cheered up the men; even Minette cried; Terrie's own eyes were moist, and many others'. The ship put out to sea at dark; solemnly its three or four searchlights played over the mother-of-pearl tenements, the villas in the hills, the feathery orchards; the shore and the breakwater were covered with silhouettes of people, waving their clothing, more and more silent, more and more sober; he could not distinguish Zizi from the rest and did not try to; never again would he see the launches come in by day or night with one sailor standing still in front, straighter than a figurehead, a flag-pole in human form, nor be that sailor; never again would he lose himself in that night full of bottles, musical instruments, kisses; he had had enough; the ship's band played "Auld Lang Syne," a few men sang.

"Well, it's a great life," his brother admitted with a mingling of two accents: one of envy of the experiences he had missed, one of profound indifference to the results of those experiences, whatever they were. "And I guess once you've been a sailor you aren't fit for much of any other life. You wouldn't have the patience."

"Well, I've got to have some fun," Terrie replied, disturbed by his brother's tone. "I got used to it. But I know one thing, I'm not going to join the navy again. I guess I'll go east and get a job."

He gazed out of the high barn-door over Wisconsin: green, sumptuous, tedious, both rich and poor at once, with little sad houses and no night-life. What was odious in it was identical with what was dear. He wanted either the violence which causes sorrow or else—no sorrow. Wisconsin mourned without having any disappointment to mourn for. Very vaguely Terrie was lonesome for temptation and regret, for sharp contrasts, for distinct good and evil—in other words, for Europe—but at the same time he hated these things from the bottom of his heart because they had made a fool of him.

Down below in the barnyard more steers, the cows, and another old horse, one before another in a procession, drew near the trough to drink. The young ones brutally pushed the others out of the way. There was a great sunbeam in the water from the setting sun. Probably it was not going to rain.

"Well," his brother went on, "I guess you might as well clear out again when we've had our visit. This ain't no place for you. You can't even get all the drink you want any more—and it's a good thing. You'd get into trouble with girls."

Terrie thought that was not what he meant; he did not want any more sweethearts, or any more drink. Nevertheless, there was a kind of thirst which, like the animals down below, he would have to quench. Wisconsin was no place for one whom its rain, its thousand of luminous creeks, its ponds, its heavy and fertile dew, failed to satisfy. Terrie had no desire to stay there on the farm with a brother who did not know enough about life to understand what he was talking about.

The Wedding March

X.

The Wedding March

In the modern cathedral the direct city sunshine was tempered by mauve and white windows. Marble of chrysanthemums had been added to the fresh walls. A large gathering was being ushered in and unfolding its elegance in the pews. The organ, restless as blooded horses held in check, preluded.

Hugo Randolph, with his best friend, came out of the vestry and took his place beside the altar. In secret he thought of this as his second wedding, though he had not been married before or even engaged, and the woman who was to that extent his bride's rival was and had been another man's wife. Fifteen years before he had been a hired man on a farm; and it was there, when the farmer and his family were away, pretending to be in search of some lost fowl, that she had come to see what he looked like at arm's-length.

Now he felt no regret; he had been a boy… Watching himself closely for his bride's sake, he believed that he was feeling no regret, impatient not only for the ceremony to be over, but for time in general to hasten on with his fortunate middle age, leaving farther and farther behind boyish excitements—ashamed and shameless, solemn, flushing and turning pale, red-eyed, jewelled with drops of sweat. In those days her husband, having bought a little farm, had gone back to bridge-building, leaving her there for months at a time; and he had been unfaithful. Hugo had had no news of her for years.

But how could he forget her—no longer young, languid but healthy, in reddish gingham that first day. A long gaze had been exchanged when his team and her little cart under an umbrella had been stopped side by side at a railroad crossing, and she had come following like a huntress the readiness, ignorance, and want which his eyes had revealed. Just out of the heat, under the live olive shadow of the hickory by the barn, she had asked irrelevant questions and he had been inarticulate. There had been a hint of husky storm in her voice and a heaviness and burning thread in the clouded look of her eyes, which had changed shape and pointed at him or at cattle in the yard or at nothing, without, under tangled eyelashes, seeming to move. One hand of a gypsy color with bright finger nails had put a strand of dark hair back. Her shoulders had held her body close and her arms had kept caressing her sides. From the first moment he had had a lump in his throat, a tension which—as if, when spoiled by awareness of itself, innocence became more precious—he had dreaded to have let loose. But he had believed then that what was beginning would never be interrupted, as long as he lived.

In the vestibule of the church he could see the four immaculate children with bouquets, awkward with a sense of responsibility and adornment, watched over by someone until the procession should form.

He would never know how, the very first morning, she had brought about a kiss. Perhaps she had not; perhaps his imagination had added to that day's pang a later comfort. Thereafter, at any rate, at night, on Sundays, upon pretexts of caring for the sheep or hunting for cattle which he had let out of pasture himself, they had met in the hills and the little warm groves. Feeling like impure fugitives until they were out of sight of houses and roads, suddenly each time they had lost track of human ideas; and love, confused with woodland vapors, with amber sunshine, muffled in flowers and branches of berries, had pretended to a virtue of its own—wholeheartedness, heedlessness, Hugo now supposed. She had never feared what might be in the grass, but pressed her cheeks and hands into it, her mouth into the damp moss; and once she had fallen asleep, with her feet, like a pair of yellowish blossoms, dabbling in the swimming hole. Naturally word of what was going on had been muttered by neighbor to neighbor, but his employers, three childless cynical pioneers, had had nothing to say so long as he got his work done; and the woman had not cared.

The wedding guests were restless and kept turning their heads back toward the door. The procession was waiting in the vestibule; the bride and her father had telephoned when they left the house, three blocks away. Someone from the vestry door must have mistaken one of the bridesmaids for the bride; the organist had begun to play the march; Hugo and the best man had come in, too soon. Something must have happened to the automobile. Now, in looser and looser variations, the march was being dispelled. Hugo's friend whispered to him.

But he was thinking that a lake had lain between his farmhouse and the house the older woman had lived in. He had tied his horse in a deserted barn and gone across in a rowboat; she had come down through a thicket. Lying back in the boat as he had rowed, she had marked the surface of the faint water with her blunt and warm fingers. He had not known what he wanted; only a sort of disorder in his eyes had made the twilight seem to come down on the lake by fits and starts. The warm fingers, still wet, had taught him to let the oars drag, had forced him not to hurry toward love.

He was in no hurry now. How could he tell how many minutes or seconds passed? He and his best man went back into the vestry. He began to feel anxiety, and felt vaguely that he might have brought bad luck upon them all by his recollections, the infidelity of his mind. But now that for a moment he needed something to think about, to pass the time, his youth failed him; he stood absent-mindedly by the vestry door with one hand on the knob. Someone who had been looking down the street ran in, and Hugo resumed his place before the attentive pews. There, as if emotion arose from the altar like some unholy evoking stone, the dancing in between present moments by hours of the past—hours of that old summer which were more brilliant and out of breath, even more solemn—began again, to the weak voluptuous march-music.

On a certain morning when the sunlight had been as glossy and leaping as the great horses at play in the barnyard, when the bouquets of fowls on the dungheaps had been like all the bloom in the fields spread out for miles around, having seen his employers go by on the road, she had visited him again. He had washed his hands and cooled off his forehead in the greenish water in the trough. He had given the young bull a drink, and she had caressed its swollen-looking russet head while he had chained it up by the ring in its nose. Then, oh, the cruel straw, and the stirring of that animal with wooden eyes, mahogany eyes, and the perfume of the stone walls, and the wisp of a cat coming and going over their heads—with a veritable rustling of his breath in his haste to expend as much of his life as could be dislodged from the close concentration of forces that youth is, to waste as much as could be wasted... But in spite of him the whole of a lifetime had been left on his hands, as he later had found to his sorrow.

There was his bride, down the aisle in the doorway out of which the bridesmaids drew back, in the familiar street which because of the dimness of the church was like a glimpse of an expanse of water, stepping out of a taxicab—thus Hugo knew that in fact it was only the automobile which had failed them—then mounting the steps like a certain amount of white and green foam, guided with one arm by the little expressive wealthy man in formal clothes.

The other woman, emphasizing often the fact of their disparate ages, which incidentally she meant to make use of to set them both free—but at the time he had not realized that, loving the man she was married to, she would want to set him free or to be free of him herself—the other woman had often described the girl he ought to seek for a wife: white, young, upon whom he could imprint his character and thus see and learn to know himself, a crystal which would not hide with too much color or mature passion the proper field of man's will-power, man's loveless and ambitious world. Thus it was she who had chosen for him fifteen years in advance the bride who in the vestibule was joining her train.

Then the wedding march started afresh, the blooded horses of the organ given the reins; but they were not swift, it was a sacramental parade not a race, they were almost like those horses in dreams which step and step without advancing. But however slowly, the soft, slight, willing girl was being carried forward by them, as certainly as a sacrifice; a sacrifice to himself and his physical beauty, of which for the first time in years it occurred to him to be proud.

He remembered how the other, laughing, had made fun of his youth, his green handsomeness, but paid tribute to it also by the storm of her breath held and let go as they sat and talked of nothing, saying almost nothing herself. And she had cried out angrily one night at the edge of the lake, and cried twice. Both her weeping and her laughter had been as if a fruit could make a sound, smooth and wet. Maybe it was actually true that her kisses had tasted of apples. Her cheeks when wet with tears had felt worn.

He was standing on a little platform, and over the girls' drooping hats he could see his bride's face through the veil, as through some tissue of hoarfrost too early a spring flower, too early in the morning. Past the dew in which his employer sat—that old man was lifting his head with a look of awe or covetousness; and in himself Hugo observed a face like an old man's, reverent and envious, lifted, not toward the present since it was in his power, but toward those memories which had come a distance of fifteen years for the occasion.

There was no chronological order in them and no development, as time, that time or this, passed. In the center of them all swirled the same sensuality, cloudy as the provoking glance had been, extravagant as in the beginning. Now he was of an age to acknowledge any physical thing shamelessly, but all the details which were passing through his mind had a color which was equivalent to blushing; or was it only the sorrow inseparable from pleasure, disguised as shame? His passion, though dead and coming back like a ghost, was only nineteen years old.

At last she had given the nineteen-year-old a rendezvous in the sheepfold, a certain sheepfold once a house and still wrapped in lilacs of a Persian color. He had spread a blanket on the springy, musky bales of wool in the loft. The most tranquil of rains had fallen on the roof. There he had told her the story of his life. "It is too short," she had complained. "Tell me another—make up one." "Your turn," he had said. Hers had been too long, any woman's life smoothed out; could it have been true? You would have said that his ardor, his youth, which were a luxury, and his hunger to take satisfying her hunger to give, had tamed and fed even the past. Any long life smoothed out by a serenity which made him shiver: he could not keep this pleasure, it did not belong to his age, they were both perishable fruit… And his imagination's tasting of death sharpened every other taste; though it was not death which would take her away.

What similarity of cadence and difference of tempo between the approach of his bride in her young rich company to the organ-music (O um di dum! O um di dum!) seemingly so long in arriving from so short a distance, and his remembering—as if the blood flowed in his veins to the same tune, but infinitely speeded up and having a dream's fullness of detail. How, between one moment in which he paid attention to the procession and the next, could he make so generous and round about an excursion into the past? It reminded him of bells which had waked him in the morning, one giving the alarm of a fire in his dream and the next sounding from the prow of a boat on its way along a profound river, one, when he was young and without hope of marrying that other woman, becoming the wedding bell toward which they walked knee-deep in roses and the next a death knell and he was left alone; although in either case he could tell by the clock that between the pairs of mechanical alarms not a minute had passed. His mind in sleep wove faster than the springs of any clock; it did now, though he was awake.

Without warning one Sunday she had said, "This is our last afternoon. We've got to say goodbye." Her husband was going to

Costa Rica to work, and she with him … "What right has he to ask you to go?" "He isn't asking. He is just letting me go. I may stay if I want to. I am afraid to. I should lose him forever. It is because I love him. You won't understand. He is the master." There had been present then the authority, even the fortitude of a man's spirit (he had been a mere boy); a scrutiny without eyes or making use of her eyes to look at him; and this evidence of a love stripped to the bone, disengaged, which was more vigorous than all their gestures, more habit-forming though less amiable than the darkness and the greensward. It had not been as a lover that he was most jealous. All the flesh of his body had gone rigid and every vein in it swelled as if it were full of wind; some evil threatened to break out of his eyes, his ears, his mouth. "Hugo, child, have I ever said that I loved you? Do you know that your fists are clenched? You aren't going to strike me —" She had smiled. Then he had burst into tears. He had never mentioned love either, but it had not occurred to him that it might not be identical with what they had enjoyed. They had been sitting on a hill on a stone-pile screened by tall, pungent, nervous poplars. He had swayed back and forth, and his tears, running uncontrollably, had made of the sunny landscape under them a vast reddish, greenish gulf. As a last resort he had tried to quarrel with her. And suddenly she had gone, and he had been too hopeless to follow, but almost immediately he had been able to stop crying and wipe his eyes. There she was, walking, running down a lane, through a stubble field, over another hill; she had thrown him a kiss.

Now he heard the brazen organ redouble its effort. Everyone was moving to one side and then standing still. His bride at arm's-length — over some girls' heads he could have touched her. The large notes of the march shrank into the pipes mechanically, like wooden saints in a cathedral clock when the hour has struck. Face to face with his blond good fortune; then they too stood shoulder to shoulder. He did not dare lift his eyes. The phrases of sacramental law; question and answer and prayer; the childish but polished hand on his without pressure; the thin, glimmering

ring; honor and obey; it was done. The stout, weary bishop gave them his blessing.

They turned, and just as they put down their feet together for the first time, the other music burst forth: a shallow, swaying, almost staggering festival, the march of the "Midsummer Night's Dream," of any common summer dream, under which everyone seemed to bow in humility, with satisfaction; venal-sounding music, out of a world in which all but two are servants.

But Hugo did not stop at once thinking of the other, the third, whom he was glad to have seen go, whose coming and going he was glad to remember. Down the slope and, like a dark bird on foot, across the fields, her spirit had left his body, which for a long while had felt dead. In the valley full of sheaves and in his youth immured... This day was an Easter for that tomb.

On his arm lay the young wife's hand; against his shoulder tossed the cloud of now purposeless veils; and the flesh of her arms and cheeks and throat looked, he thought, as her drooping, trailing bouquet smelled. For the wedding ceremony, working like some rite of more specific magic, had raised also from the dead, out from under the masonry which in his ambitious, well-disciplined bachelor's heart he had laid to keep it down — love. Love, the repeatedly dead. It would also rise repeatedly, even in the city nights, again and again unprohibited, and be made as before of gold foliage and shepherd's musk, blood-heat and sprinkle of tears. So that his bride's unfriendly purity, like some too early hour of the day, would blush, and her eyes of common forget-me-not blue cloud with a more desirable, animated warmth; for it was still midsummer and noon that he loved most in women.

The rest of that long-ago summer and fall, and shorter and shorter memorial periods of the years which followed, had been miserable in the other woman's honor. That idyll like another had been mightier in retrospect than while it had taken place; so much more fleeting are all actions, so much more evanescent the body, than illusions and the mind. Youth is a day during which one cannot keep wide awake, a night during which one cannot sleep,

Hugo thought; one has too much imagination at a certain age. The nineteen-year-old filling the hollow of his desire with harvest of pictures, books and others' shamelessness, with memories if he has any (he had had those): a soft whirring of slight machines of flesh, the dimness that rises from a threshing floor, sheaves beaten, choking yellow chaff bit by bit blown away, and at last—it takes too long—the few grains of bodily habit separated and gathered up in the grown man's hand...

He was glad, grown man in pursuit and in possession of wealth that he was, that mature life afforded less opportunity for thought and more time for doing, which leaves the brain unhaunted, the heart light. But it was a good thing that the woman he was now almost ready to forget had taught him what was the equivalent of long thought about the intoxications that do not originate with drink or drug; about separation which is a working model of death; about the way two truths such as her two unquestionable passions may coincide or overlap; about love in which pleasure has been worn thin or worn entirely away, love dismembered of jealousy and obedience and all question of any change of heart, love that is no less than a destiny by which one soul is doomed to another, in the path of which is rapidly swept aside what a woman may feel for any boy.

By this time he and his bride and the company following had come to the door and went happily down into the street and so back to their daily lives. Behind them in the great church whose walls on the inside were the color of a tomb, the organ-music folded about the steps they had all taken and faded away.

The Whistling Swan

XI.

The Whistling Swan

Hubert Redd sat staring at the piano in his mother's home. A chromo of St. Cecilia—face upturned toward a cluster of angels, unsuitable tapering hands on the keyboard of an invisible instrument—had always hung above it. It was an upright of Western make, the varnish slightly blistered long ago, the middle C and G below it chipped; no new damage had been done while he had been abroad. Probably it had not even been touched; his mother had kept it in tune, she said, because she had faith in her boy and knew that one fine day he would come home. In his childhood, after dark when the chores were done, he had sometimes cried because milking made his fingers too stiff to play and because he was too young to be taken seriously, with a poor father who could not believe that a living might be made by music, in a country where the piano was thought suitable only to unmarried women; then he had been consoled by the romantic tears which fell directly on the keys if he held his head at a certain angle, and had memorized his first piece in order to be able to play when the notes melted and drew off in that distress which resembled a light, swirling cloud.

That was in another part of the state, before his parents had come north in search of prosperity. After his grandfather's lumberyards in Prospect, a suburb of Milwaukee, had been sold in order to divide the inheritance among four brothers, his father had tried farming, unsuccessfully, and later had moved to this lumbering town, Woodland, hoping to profit by his early experience. That also had been a disappointment; having invested all he had in a sawmill, he was now employed as a sort of foreman by the larger mill which had driven it into bankruptcy; the mother had explained their misfortune to her son.

Hubert had returned from Europe because the allowance a Chicago banker had been sending him had been discontinued. He was not sure that his parents would have helped him even if they had been able to afford to; though there was no question of his staying long in that town, it would be a great comfort to his mother, now that her health was failing, to have him somewhere in their own country which she understood, in which she could picture to herself his daily life. Fortunately he did not have to explain to her the reason for his return. She hoped that in part, perhaps unconsciously, he had been drawn back to Wisconsin by love of more than one kind, and that when she and his father let him go again, they would have to give up Muriel Pater as well. This girl had already been called his sweetheart when they were children, and soon after he had gone abroad and his parents moved to Woodland, had got employment there in the lumber company's offices. Mrs. Redd told her son what a pleasure it had been for them to reread together all of her letters and part of Muriel's, evidently drawing her own conclusions from the fact that the girl skipped paragraphs or entire pages.

Life had made him a gift of this girl. Originally he had loved her for her sympathy, that is, loved himself through her as well as in other ways. After he went abroad he had written, every week, not perfectly truthful records of his feeling, but love-letters of the man he hoped to become to the girl he would have chosen; a sensitive needle must have some pole to turn to. Then, having addressed so many pages to his own idealism, he dreaded seeing the real Muriel again. But she had profited by every phrase, imitated every compliment, prepared herself to meet strange expectations. Failing to love her now would be unfaithfulness not only to her, but to a work of his imagination.

Hubert Redd looked out of the window, then brought a pile of scores out of his bedroom and put them on the piano, but went back to the window. The ten-year-old town lay open to the autumn forest; in any direction he could see a bit of its torn unclean edge. The river, already swollen, completely covered the dam; it was discolored by sawdust. Hubert was not used to seeing Scandinavian faces, red uneven foreheads and pale eyes which pointed nowhere. All of it somehow suggested crime; he did not know whether that was because it was the setting of a certain type of motion picture or because of the wreckage of exploitation everywhere: a sort of slaughter-house, stumps and stumps and prostrate branches, a festering of weeds where there must have been clean ferns and club moss, the evil effect heightened by the bright colors of the season, red branches in a slaughter-house. And the wood still bleeding gently in four-square piles was not fine enough for musical instruments or any other beautiful use; summer bungalows, endless copies of the ugliest imaginable chair, newspaper…

When he sailed from France he had believed it to be for a short visit only. Then he had thought eagerly of his parents' new home. The northern forest, scarcely hunted in, astir with large birds, echoing purely with an unwritten, unknown sonority; every sight, even the wild stags and the young bears in the rhythmic foliage, would mean sound; he would work under a spell, and to cover the ruled paper he had brought along would come a jet of free, clear, clean music. As a matter of fact, since he had been at home, he had not seen anything extraordinary or heard anything but song-sparrows; instead there were whistles and wheels, the harsh feverish purring of the dam, the saws' incessant scream, low at the start like something in the bone behind one's ear, rising to a hideous note, choking on it and fading down the scale, over and over all day long; and he had no lofty sentiments about machines.

In any case, the fact that he might have to stay on indefinitely in America gave him so much to think about that he could not expect himself to work at once. His patron, instead of sending the usual quarterly check, had suggested a visit home, offering to pay his expenses—later chuckling over this trick. Hubert had accepted, the ocean fare had come and he had taken the earliest second-class boat.

Upon his arrival in Chicago he had telephoned to Mr. Crawley's offices and been given an appointment. As he had stepped out of the elevator a bald young man waiting beside the door marked Private had beckoned him down the corridor, one finger on his lips. "I am Mr. Graver, the secretary. You remember me, we met in Paris. How are you? Come with me a minute."

He had hurried him into another elevator and out of it into a booth in an ice-cream parlor on the first floor. "Excuse me for seizing upon you. I wanted to tell you—it is only fair—besides, it may help you. Of course you must realize, in spite of whatever has happened, that Mr. Crawley is a splendid man, kindly, open-minded, and idealistic, and he is very fond of you. You have been perhaps—I do not say certainly—indiscreet, not so far as he is concerned, I mean toward Mrs. Crawley. Indeed there has been some discussion between them on the subject, and she once took me into her confidence to the extent of asking me to use my slight influence on her side. I may tell you, between you and me, that Mr. Crawley has also been indiscreet. She has a jealous nature—"

Hubert had had time to wonder if the strangely amiable young man was deranged, but not—in the stream of obscure phrases uttered in a frivolous but melancholy tone, scanned by gestures with a handkerchief and rapid glances here and there—to put in a phrase of his own.

"Very jealous—and when she returned from Europe this last time there were, about the house you understand, certain tell-tale objects; one or two malicious gossips in Oak Park where they live also did their work—Mr. Crawley admitted as much to me personally—and of course she was then in a position to demand anything she wanted. She wanted your head; just like Salome in the opera if I may say so; indeed I think she went abroad this last time with that in mind."

"You must be mistaken, Mr. Graver. Mrs. Crawley was particularly kind to me last June. I went with her everywhere and she asked me to introduce my friends to her."

"Oh no, worse luck, I am not mistaken. I hoped you would understand better than you do." He glanced at his wrist-watch. "Now you must hurry up to the office. These are delicate matters."

"I am late already," Hubert had said irritably.

"No, you are not late. I gave you an appointment ten minutes before Mr. Crawley would be free, hoping to have a word with you. Now if there is ever anything I personally can do for you…"

Hubert had been ushered into the great, shaded inner room: thick green carpet, mahogany and plump leather, Whistler etchings on the walls, a fireplace full of gilt leaves. The great banker, flushed, with unusually liquid eyes, would have been handsome if his face had matured as it had aged; he had that gentle nervousness which often accompanies business men's diseases, but on this occasion had not risen from the least luxurious chair in the room.

"Young man," he had said, "I have no questions to ask you. This is unpleasant for us both. But if you will be patient and not interrupt me, you shall hear how things stand. Mrs. Crawley and I are unsatisfied with your behavior. It is not a question of music. We don't pretend to be competent to judge modern efforts along that line. The symphony concerts, Wagner and Beethoven, have meant a lot to us. We have a debt, and we like to pay somebody for what we enjoy. Leave that out of this. This has to do with character. I didn't want to dictate all this to my stenographers."

He had spoken coldly but uneasily. "Do me justice. I paid your passage back." It was then that he had chuckled. "I saw no reason why you should deprive Mrs. Crawley over there of the credit that is due her for the interest she has taken in you. By getting somebody else to take care of you, I mean, temporarily. We sent you over there. Now we are back where we began."

He had hurried over the words which followed. "Now, my boy, that is the last financial assistance you are to expect. It has gone on long enough. Two years it's been, hasn't it? Mind you, I am not speaking of your work. It is probably very fine. I don't pretend to be a connoisseur…"

Unreasonable as one may be on such occasions, Hubert kept thinking: this means that I shall never meet Stravinsky, what I wanted most, my last chance. Nothing helped him to give it up: neither what he had heard about his disposition, his earnest malice and locked Russian courtesy, nor the fact that only imitation musicians made an object of such meetings, nor the possibility that instead of playing himself the great man might ask him to and that his hard attention like that of a bird with a powerful brain, a bird out of the *Arabian Nights,* might let him know that all he had done was bad; no matter what happened, for he felt sure that there were in himself resources which he had not been able to open up and only wished for something or someone to break through to them, to tear as it were a certain membrane, to remove an obstruction in his imagination's speech; and at the first-night of the "Odipus" oratorio, when all magnificent-looking Paris had listened as if to a poorly performed revival of Händel or Rossini, after it was over, on the steps of the dirty old theater, there had come to his eyes tears rather of exasperated desire than of emotion roused by the masterpiece with its rigidity of extreme sentiments lacking tears…

"Now I sent you regularly," Mr. Crawley had continued, "a good living. In fact, Mrs. Crawley when she was in Paris learned, and from friends of yours, that the same amount would have supported two artists. She might have had two chances in the lottery, she said. But that wasn't enough for your luxurious tastes. My wife learned that you have been accepting money as well from young Mrs. Jack Rohan. I have had business dealings with her husband. I don't want to be misunderstood. I mean to speak to him about this matter. Don't worry, I shall be strictly fair. Apparently she makes quite a business of patronizing. Apparently she dropped one of her young poets for your benefit. He has my sympathy."

Hubert had had an impression that the financier was trying to remember things he had been told to say, to take the place of something he was not going to speak of.

"Now we have no objection," he had said, "to your writing something when you feel inclined, provided it's along musical lines. But if you do a thing, do it well. The same young poet told my wife that a very important editor—you know his name if I don't, a greater man than you are, you must admit—had turned down your criticisms because they were laughable and because your dealings were so underhanded."

Hubert had begun to pay less attention to what his benefactor said than to the people he mentioned, the confused memories which corresponded one by one to the articles of his denunciation: the light-hearted woman who had provided him with costly scores and some unnecessary clothes; the great theorist and editor, incessant anecdotes in a voice like a flute, a virile bearded body somewhere in the center of which the malice of an old Massachusetts woman sat in judgment; the young California poet, eight of whose verses he had memorized: phantoms merely set in motion in cafés and studios and revolutionary concerts but who had their real life here in the West at his heels. And a strange fear, keyless and meterless and with great round notes, a sort of choir of cryptic accusations, of secrets which at any moment might swell enough to be heard by anyone who was interested, began to make him shrink down in the overstuffed chair; he had forgotten that Paris and Chicago were suburbs one of the other; and only politeness toward the aging gentleman to whom he had to be grateful for the finest things in his life had kept him from putting his fingers in his ears...

"There was even worse talk about Paris than this. Mrs. Crawley was shocked. I find it very disagreeable to speak of it at all. I do not wish to ask you any questions. Some of the company you keep is evidently the worst. People get degenerate from having too much time on their hands. Young men and women with very morbid minds—I am surprised they are not in sanatoriums. Sensation hunters, decadents, there is no doubt of it. I am not accusing you of anything. Mrs. Crawley did not care to hear. That is strictly your business." He raised his head and his mellow voice grew proud like a public speaker's. "But we people in the West don't need to ask for information. We draw our own conclusions. We can afford to. Even if we do make mistakes."

Hubert wondered why he had not risen some time before. "Mr. Crawley, I will say goodbye. I thank you for all that you have done for me. Please remember me respectfully to Mrs. Crawley. I am going to Wisconsin tonight."

"That is the place for you. Home to your father. A simple old-fashioned home. I may be a rich man, but I have reverence, a genuine reverence, for poverty. Maybe I am to blame for having accustomed you to a life of idleness. Please believe that I meant well. My love of music led me astray."

Apparently by this time he believed every word of his indictment. "My boy, you have had things too easy." His voice broke slightly; his eyes were suffused with a glistening pinkness. "Let me tell you, the most wonderful thing in life is to make sacrifices. For your duty and your honor. And sacrifices to your family. I shall go on doing it. Don't you regret your life over there abroad. Let me tell you, there is nothing in it. Do take responsibility now and settle down. And try to be grateful to Mrs. Crawley and me, even if we can't see our way clear to helping you any more."

"Mr. Crawley, goodbye. I must go, if you please."

The excited man had not seemed to want him to, but he had looked content and tired out. He had also had the lost look which all martyrs to duty and domestic affection have when they are alone.

In the corridor Hubert had shivered involuntarily, though his mingled pity and dread of his benefactor had been a warmer emotion than any he had felt before. He had seen but pretended not to see Mr. Graver, feeling like a small boy who dares not relax his throat lest the sounds aching in it be unmanly. He had taken the first train north; it had seemed appropriate to his distress to sit up all night. At that time he had firmly intended to write Mrs. Jack Rohan an account of the rupture and a direct request to help him return to Paris.

As soon as he got home he had written to the old woman who, as his teacher, had presented him to the Crawleys; unperturbed, she had replied with an offer of a position in the music department of a small college south of Milwaukee. He was still putting off the letter to Mrs. Rohan, perhaps out of desire to avoid knowing if Mr. Crawley's accusations had reached her ears or, childishly, to keep the possibility of her help as a refuge for his thought, when disheartenment went too far. Something was happening to him in the north; it was not inspiration; it was not love, though Muriel wove around him the spell of hers, never foolish, never tactless, disheartened by nothing…

His mother came into the room. "I met your girl down-town, and she asked me to tell you that she is coming over about one o'clock. It's Saturday, you know, so she's free." She made a more tidy pile of his music on the piano. "I've been thinking… It seems to me you're not quite so cheerful after you've been with her."

"Silly mother. She is my dearest friend in the world."

"That may be. Friendship isn't love." She put her hands on his shoulders. "Look here, son. You mustn't let us railroad you into marrying her if, in your heart of hearts… It's hard for mothers and sweethearts, you know, to put themselves in another's place. Muriel is a dear daughter to me. But I only want you to be happy. And I hope she loves you no less than that."

At the end of the noonday meal, there Muriel stood in the doorway: moderate beauty, womanly, white, and healthy, blue-clad. For some reason, though she was only twenty-six, her hair was turning; it was like a silver-fox pelt and almost too fine to be pleasant to touch. "Here am I, the lumberjack." She sank into the chair nearest the piano. "Mrs. Redd, look the other way. I'm going to smoke."

They sat there and said nothing of importance. She knew why he had come home and urged him to write to Mrs. Rohan, even to the Dutch ambassador's wife at whose concerts his best work had been played; but so bitter was her fear of being left behind again that her voice grew unnaturally ardent and low. Under her placid eyebrows her eyes, small and pure in color, obstinate and sweet, never left his face. He was ill at ease; he could not wish for her to stay all afternoon, though he tried, and charged himself with innate coldness. But a few days before she had said, "I know that your feeling is not comparable to mine, but, Hubert, so little of your love would be enough…" Between one and another went something that resembled a violin string which an invisible finger incessantly stroked and made to vibrate—a fretful monotone of love weakly sustained. Hubert listened, listened, could hear only that, and could not hear the future say a thing.

His mother came into the room. "You must play all your best pieces for Muriel. I'll sit out on the porch and listen."

Muriel was grateful not to have had to ask. Hubert adjusted the swivel stool and opened the keyboard. He wished Muriel would not put out her cigarette and clasp her hands. He played five extremely brief two-part sonatas, the material of the first not only varied in the second according to the tradition, but made to accompany a new phrase and its development. The outworn piano frightened him, but he played well enough: nude, fresh, percussive sound. Between the third and the fourth outside the window the creak of his mother's rocking-chair stopped and deep breathing began; later she retired to the back of the house. Muriel closed her eyes and her eyelids fluttered.

Hubert stood up. She did so as well, and rested her hands and chin on the poor old instrument. "They are beautiful, beautiful. As beautiful as Mozart—that's what you like best, isn't it? I can't tell you how much they mean to me. Your mother went to sleep; they ought not to be played in Wisconsin. I think Paris must be like them, phenomenal, exotic, all in a certain style and almost painful. Even Debussy is not as strange…" She spoke with a touching effort.

Then Hubert saw all their faults. Only self-consciousness kept him from hunting out the manuscript and tearing it up. Was this not mere perversity—to react to excessive and loving praise with disparagement of himself? Would her appreciation always make him detest what he had done? Perhaps it was a way of making her responsible for his weak work, for his weakness in general. He was ashamed of himself. He kissed her pale forehead.

Then he said, "I want to go for a walk in the woods now." He spoke a little bluntly; it was imperative to be alone.

"You mean that you don't want me along?"

"Forgive me. I have thought of a song and I want to think about it some more." The classic lie…

He went upstairs after his father's rifle; he might bring home something to eat. He heard Muriel call, "Mrs. Redd, our young man is going out composing. In the woods. I'll take a nap and then help get supper if I may stay."

"Keep the big hills to the right on your way along, and to the left coming back, and you won't get lost," his mother replied from somewhere.

"You look very desperate with your gun," Muriel said.

"Can you see me desperate? I might make better music if I were."

While he was in sight she was watching him. As usual, he was trying to make up his mind what to do; he did not believe in resigning himself to circumstances. Composers never made a living wage—all the opulence, century after century, going to the performers—but there was no use in his trying to give concerts: his hands were the wrong shape, too much like those of St. Cecilia over the piano, and in general he was not sturdy enough to stand touring and did not enjoy public appearances enough to make capital of fatigue, nerves, and fever, as many of the young Slavs did. There was no cheap leisure in America; he had no desire even to hear the music that could be made out of weary living, aspiration, scraps of time, his own or anyone else's. And in a Western music school he would lose himself in a swarm of mediocre youngsters, envying them their age; and honor would oblige him to offer them the principles that other musicians had proved to be true rather than those he had hoped to add to the number, and to prefer their first efforts to his last…

Forlornly he had put off writing to Mrs. Rohan in order not to risk his last chance, not to gamble on reality with his last illusion, until now it had become habitual to lack the courage to do so; he wondered how much or how little she cared about music or about him, remembering her zest for novelty, her timidity in any dispute (and by this time Mr. Crawley would have had his word with her husband), her Western accent and soft voice like that of a Michigan Boulevard pigeon; she forgot like a Parisian and like an American; he had been but a three days' wonder and it was some one else's turn. All over, done for. If he had in him the makings of a great musician (and there had never been great music in America) it was a pity; if not, what did it matter to anyone but himself?

Meanwhile he had made his way into the forest by a rough road, among softening stumps on which superb, discolored funguses fed, over chips and broken limbs, the town gradually slipping behind groups of large trees which had been spared and behind feathery thickets of new growth; the autumn not only unrolling softly from north to south in the sky, speckled with birds also going south, but signing itself everywhere—a wash of blues between him and the range of hills, marks brightly painted on the small vegetation, a mere look of weariness in the tall hemlocks. Presently he turned down a pathway where logs must have been dragged along, then down another, avoiding the clearings; it was the deep untouched forest, if there was any left, which he sought, feeling newly stripped of every rare quality himself—and of that which is commonplace only the primitive seemed to have any enchantment, dignity, or peace…

If only he had been, if he could have resigned himself to be, a mere young man not driven by ambition, not elected or self-appointed to a special destiny, not overwrought with one talent! Personally, his hopes of becoming a musician set aside, he would not regret Paris. The first winter, wet and dim, when so far as he was concerned the crowds had been nameless to the last illustrious or ratlike man; a city as plain and august as the pots in the Orient out of which flowering plants are supposed to spring before one's eyes, with boulevards of secretive luxury, with dank honeycombs to live in and hoarse janitors keeping watch, with warm meeting-places of innumerable foreigners, with apparent folly and semblances of eccentric scholarship; the dream-Paris of Gerard de Nerval who was hanged on a lamp-post, and his own first spring there coming on like a fever, like love: then and only then it had seemed all prodigy and allurement. But promptly this ideal nightmare resolved itself into reasonable elements; he began to profit as a musician by Paris and, as a human being, to pay for the strict sobriety of its attention to the arts and the invaluable loneliness of the foreign artist in the close-packed, intelligent crowd. He learned to know its penury of tenderness, its need or craving for narcotics, apostasies, and revolutions in dumb-show; the pleasures flavored with piety and remorse; the deceptive wit of its great men, the irresponsible skill devoted to manipulating youth; the aristocratic combinations of bankruptcy with extravagance, the complex parasitism (Hubert realized that he was accusing his friends as his patron had accused him), the shamelessness without candor, the skepticism of panic underlying brilliant opinions. The more tolerance, the less warm enthusiasm—or so it seemed. A banquet table at which, on the whole, one goes hungry for the sake of certain foods; a little nourishment and many drugs—such is the world's hospitality. Nevertheless, Hubert resolved to write Mrs. Rohan that night about returning to Paris.

So he went along through the woods carrying his gun, but when he saw two or three partridges like dwarfs in brocade and aigrettes walking and talking to each other, he could not take aim in time, the sight of them too pleasing to leave him any presence of mind. Where the sun made its way between branches both of tree and cloud, grew small rough flowers covered with bees; juniper spread out its great crowns of fur and wire and berries; and having walked a long way, he came upon strong-smelling, swampy hollows. The growth was dense, but he was not satisfied; for here and there he came upon stumps or ominous marks of the axe on mature trees, and his path still seemed to have a destination. He said to himself that he did not like this country because it was merely in the process of becoming what other countries were perfectly. Would not staying there, for any such craftsman or inventor as a musician, be perversely going back to the beginning instead of starting where others had left off?

But if he stayed, he added, and taught in a college, the anxiety which his feeling for Muriel had turned into would be brought to an end. Her love that was or was not his creation, his love with its attendant ideal of himself which he surely had created, detail by detail like a piece of music—he did not know what to do with them, and in Europe would never know. He loved her, but did not need her. In the life of a music-teacher in Wisconsin, need, compound and constant, would supplant all the other emotions.

All the way along, his over-sensitive ear of its own accord had gathered up and disentangled and, as it were, commented upon the innumerable sounds of the forest; now, fascinated, he began to be unable to withhold his entire attention, began almost to suffer from them: great sagging clusters of vague tones, a slumbering, tossing, and sighing in slumber, sound for the eye as well as the ear—he heard but did not see sluggish currents of autumn and short ripples with which winter was beginning, and amid wind and wood, other leaves and small echoes, saw but could not hear the arpeggio of a maple hand sweeping the width of some stringed instrument—a beak beating on hollow wood, the senseless rhythm of his feet crumpling leaves, breaking twigs, and an increasing vibration high in key of marsh insects some distance off, less and less far off; all this palpitating mass of marrying, dividing notes seeming to lead up to something and then breaking down of its own weight; suddenly the long, watery, over-ripe phrase of some bird... It was music, all too musical, but of a style which was passing—too closely related to too many sounds, too far removed from easy speech and tragic outcry both.

Hubert thought that he was approaching a clearing. Instead he came out on the shores of a lake. Pale, very little rippled, it lay under slopes and bulky trees. Its breath was cold. Its vast extent made an almost complete silence. The shore was swathed in tawny thickets, the shallows full of reeds, but there was a firm water's edge. Hubert amused himself by following it. He jumped from one solid piece of sod to another, as softly as he could in order to hear the little sigh of roots, bubbles, and soil under him. He did not care if he got his feet wet. Lest his gun get caught in the brush and overhanging branches, he pointed it ahead. Perhaps he might see a pair of sunfish close to land. He would have to go round a small bay …

Suddenly an enormous bird sprang up in front of him. Very close, pale wings thrashing, long neck outthrust—that was all he saw. Terribly startled, he shot it. It broke down into the water, dragging itself away. He dropped his gun and stood with his arms out as if he were going to fall on his hands and knees. He could not see it; a bush in the water covered it up. There was a terrific splashing. Then it screamed. He had thought they were dumb, all the swans, he had thought they were dumb. The scream went on and changed and did not stop. In despair at dying, it whistled, whistled, and took its breath. Broken open, a heavy stream of music let out—but it was the opposite of music. Now husky, now crude, what were like clots of purity often, the rhythm of something torn. Greater beating of the wings, greater agony of the splashes, whipping, kicking. He was being made to hear what it would have been insufferable to see. Sudden silence. The water was dirty and red.

Hubert squatted on the wet shore and began to cry, but stopped because the sound of his voice was ludicrous. He did not want to see what was left of the swan. It was mere fright that had made him kill it; but if he had not been frightened he would not have heard its cries. He felt a sick satisfaction, definite jealousy of the dead bird, an extreme feebleness, a great haste.

He picked up the gun because it was his father's, and hurried home. Wisconsin had changed; it had become the scene of what had just happened. He would be held there by magnetism, that sometimes exercised by trysting place or tomb, about which, almost content with his apparent loss, the lover wanders in hope of some ghost with relaxed plumage and forgotten voice; that exercised, for men who love themselves, by the spots marked with a cross where something they once were fell dead. Well then, he would stay — but not to express his native land in music. He would make them hear what it would be either unendurable to experience or on earth impossible to find. Or he would hold his peace — a dumb, wholesome, personal peace. Talk about Paris, who cared, who cared?... That night he accepted the offer of the college in the south of the state, and agreed with Muriel to be married at once.

Previous Publication of Glenway Wescott's Stories

"Goodbye, Wisconsin" appeared in *New York Herald Tribune Books*, July 1928.

Versions of "The Runaways" appeared in *Collier's National Weekly*, July 4, 1925; *The Best Short Stories of 1925*; and *A Twentieth Century Anthology of Modern Literature*, 1930.

"A Guilty Woman" appeared in *Century*, August, 1928; *The Best Short Stories of 1928, Neue Schweizer Rundschau*, August 1929; and *Neu Amerika*, 1937.

"The Dove Came Down" appeared in *Harper's Magazine*, April 1928; and *Contemporary Trends: American Literature Since 1914*, 1933.

"Like a Lover" appeared in *la revue européene*, May 1928; and privately published.

"In a Thicket" appeared in *The Dial*, June 1924; *The Best Short Stories of 1924*, and *la revue européene*, July 1934.

"Prohibition" appeared in *Harper's Magazine*, October 1927; and *O. Henry Memorial Award Prize Stories of 1928*.

"The Sailor" appeared in *American Harvest*, 1942; and *Crazy Mixed-up Kids*, 1955.

"The Whistling Swan" appeared in *The Bookman*, June 1928.

Colophon

This book is set in Sabon, an old style serif typeface designed by the German-born typographer and designer Jan Tschichold (1902–1974). It was designed by Ken Crocker, and printed and bound by Worzalla Publishing Company.

	DATE DUE